The Perfect Christmas

BARBARA WINKES

ISBN: 978-1-0696671-3-7

For D.

Chapter One

ANGIE

To Angie Winters, family mattered the most. Christmas was a close second. Creating the perfect holiday required meticulous planning, and her loved ones assured her each year that she was more than up to the task.

As rewarding as she found the joy in their eyes, something was different this year, she reflected as she left work and stepped into a blizzard, or so it felt. The snow was coming down hard.

She should be home right now, mixing cookie dough, writing cards, and checking their wrapping paper supply, among many other things. Angie hoped that Neva, her wife, had gotten a head start on the cookies. They still had multiple boxes to fill, and this was only one item on her ever-expanding to-do list.

With one of her colleagues being sick at home, and another one new to the job, there was no way she could have left the office early. She still had to pick up her gift for Neva, a handmade, customized piece of jewelry she had commissioned from a local jeweler to mark their fifteenth Christmas together.

Without question, this year had to be *extra* special.

It would be, right after she dealt with a few more inconveniences. Driving around the small shopping center's parking garage without finding a spot, she couldn't help the rising frustration.

Only two weeks, and there was still so much to do. She was lucky that Neva, who worked from home, could help the kids with their homework, and address any immediate crisis, but she, too, had a job to do.

It meant that dishes sometimes stayed in the sink until the next day, or dust settled on surfaces. And that was without a major holiday—*the* holiday—only a couple of weeks away. Neva had a small studio, but she hadn't been able to make time to paint in some time.

Christina, Fiona, and Elsa helped out, but along with school, they had their own social lives, and Angie didn't want to interfere too much. Above all, she wanted everyone in their home to be happy, and she was determined to succeed, even if it meant she would collapse in a heap on the couch on Christmas Eve.

No, come to think of it, that was not possible, given that they were hosting both sets of parents on Christmas Day. She might sleep for a couple of days straight after that day, but until then, she would make sure it would be the perfect celebration.

Her and Neva's anniversary. The twins Fiona and Elsa's birthday. Everyone they loved under one roof. What could be better? It was truly the most wonderful time of the year.

She sighed in relief when another shopper pulled out of their parking spot, only for that spot to be taken before she could move in.

Relax. Take a deep breath. Angie took pride in the fact that she neither yelled at the other driver, nor used a swear word, but turned around and left the parking garage instead.

The snowfall had intensified, and when she finally found a spot on the curb, she nearly ended up with one wheel on the sidewalk.

Angie headed back to the shopping center's front doors, waiting for the familiar effect. It never came. While she appreciated the heat inside, the sounds of Christmas music, children's laughter, and the warm scents of baked goods did nothing to calm her.

This was her favorite season. She loved the organizing, the hunt for the perfect presents and decorations, and the way it all came together for unforgettable moments of joy and peace. Every year. This year would be no exception.

Angie wasn't going to allow a little exhaustion to impede her plans. She had lists, detailed lists, many of them. Perhaps she could manage to take a day off before...

"You've got to be kidding me," she said out loud when she stood in front of the jeweler's door. The store was dark, a sign left on the closed door.

We had to close early due to an emergency. We are sorry and will be back tomorrow.

Tomorrow? She did feel bad for the jeweler who was a well-known and beloved artist in town, but...There was no way Angie could come back tomorrow. After the workday, she had planned to make headway on the gift-wrapping, and finish planning the menu for the next grocery.

She might be able to leave some of that to Neva...or not. While the latter was the most kind and beautiful soul Angie had ever met, she wasn't much of a cook. Or a planner.

Angie loved her with all her heart. Regardless, some of the items on the list—lists—still had to be done by her and her alone. She had managed each of those fourteen years before, and even when she was younger and had full control over her parents' home and decorations for the holidays.

She took out her cell phone, only to find a text message from Nadine, the jeweler.

I'm so sorry, she wrote. *There was a burst pipe at my home, and I had to close the store. You can pick up your order tomorrow morning or at lunch, whatever works for you.*

The message had come in during Angie's search for a parking space. Why hadn't she checked earlier? She could be home right now.

Did you all have dinner yet? she texted Neva.

The answer came right away, full of heart emojis that made her smile.

Yes, but don't worry, we left you some. We have a surprise for you.

Emojis aside, the tension that had almost dissipated was about to return full force. With this little time to spare to get everything done, Angie didn't care much for surprises. If she was honest, she didn't care for them most of the time.

It didn't matter. She had to head home and adjust her plans. First, she sent an encouraging message to Nadine and promised she would come back for the necklace. Her text to Neva was a blatant lie, but it was all she could do at the moment:

Can't wait!

Great. See you soon? Love you.

Love you too. That was nothing but the truth. There was nothing she was more certain of. Angie hoped it would make up for the other part, and that the surprise wouldn't throw off the evening schedule too much.

She passed the bakery again on the way back out, tempted. Angie resisted, not wanting to disappoint her family who had left some of the dinner she and Neva had prepared the other day.

Driving home, Angie listened to her favorite Christmas mix, on constant replay in her car for all of Advent. Some people disliked it. It usually centered her, though not tonight. This late in the evening, traffic should be light, but it was close to Christmas, and the heavy snowfall had slowed down late commuters almost to a stop.

It meant she would have dinner while the first batch of cookies was in the oven.

Maybe Neva's surprise meant that they were all done already.

The fantasy helped carry her all the way home.

It was almost a miracle that she had made it safely in this weather. There was always something to be grateful for, Angie mused as she made her way to the front door. The cookies could wait a few more minutes. She was hungry, and she wanted to change into something warm and comfortable first.

If the snow didn't let up overnight, she would have to add some shoveling to the agenda. She would deal with that tomorrow. She noticed that two of the colorful lights in the string decorating the fir in the front had burned out. Another item for the list.

All the lights were on in the house, decorations in the window a bit crooked, but giving the place a welcoming appearance. It made her smile. Coming home to her family was the best part of the day, not just at this time of the year.

Angie unlocked the door and went inside only to be greeted enthusiastically by their two dachshunds, Bert and Ernie. They jumped up and down, demanding to be petted.

"Guys. Relax."

"Mommy!" The humans had caught up on her arrival as well, and Fiona and Elsa joined her in the hallway. Angie noticed that neither of them was in PJs yet. To her disappointment, the house didn't smell like cookies either.

"Hey. Did you have a good day?" She gathered the twins close, assuming that Christina was upstairs video-chatting with a friend or reading.

"The best!" Fiona claimed. "You won't believe what happened. We have a—"

"A kitten," Angie finished her sentence, staring at the tiny bundle in disbelief. There was no doubt though. The bundle meowed. When did that happen?

"*Neva*?"

"Right here."

Neva stood in the doorway, regarding the scene with unmistakable affection and pride. Angie, too, was proud of their family, their babies, human and fur...She had not expected this spontaneous addition, especially when they were so busy. She pressed two fingers against her temple, feeling a headache build.

"Can we keep her, Mommy? Mama said we should ask you. If you say yes, you can name her."

"That's very kind of you." Angie straightened and looked from the pleading eyes of her child clutching the kitten to her now apologetic wife. "Can we talk for a second?"

"Of course. Let's go in the kitchen. I'll heat up your dinner."

"Mommy?"

"I'll think about it," she called. "Mama and I need to have a word."

In the kitchen, she slumped into a chair and dropped her purse on the one next to her.

Neva fixed a plate for Angie and put it in the microwave.

"I can explain," she said. "Amanda called this morning. They found a home for all of the kittens but one..."

Angie distantly remembered that Amanda, Neva's sister, had been fostering a litter of kittens.

"And you thought this was a good idea?"

"Amanda can't keep her, and we didn't want her to go to a shelter. Bert and Ernie seem to like her well enough, and the kids are already in love. What do you say?"

She had many things to say. Angie would hold them back until after she had eaten, changed, and baked a couple of sheets of cookies. At least. Once she'd accomplished all of that, it would be easier to accept that she was likely going to lose the argument.

Three children, two dogs. Now they wanted to introduce a kitten into the mix? Impossible. It didn't look like she had much of a say in the matter though.

"There you go." Neva, sounding hopeful, set the steaming plate in front of her. Crispy chicken, steamed vegetables, and mashed potatoes.

"Thank you. We're going to need a new string of lights for the tree outside, and check if the ones for inside are all functioning. Oh, and the wrapping paper. Did you check if we have enough?"

"Not yet, but I'll do that tomorrow. I promise."

"Good. I'll get started on the cookies as soon as I'm done. I'd like to have that out of the way. What's wrong?" she asked, concerned, when Neva's expression became somber.

"I don't know, the way you said it..."

"How did I say it? We have a lot to do."

Don't go there. All she wanted was to scratch a few more items off the list. Her work situation or the snowstorm weren't Neva's fault. Angie had no reason to snap at her.

"I know that," Neva acknowledged. "I just want you to enjoy the season, too."

"I am, don't worry." How was that even a question? She wouldn't be doing all this if she didn't enjoy it, would she? She was looking forward to this all year. Angie was starting to get impatient with herself. She needed to manage her time better. "Is it true that I can name the kitten?"

"Of course you can." Neva took her hand and held it in hers. "Thank you for this. They were smitten the moment they saw her. I swear, there was nothing I could do."

"I know the feeling."

When Neva's lips curved into a smile, Angie knew she didn't have to elaborate.

"All right. This one can stay, but we agree that's it, right? No more additional occupants after Fluffy?"

"Fluffy?" Neva's voice went up a notch. "I'm already regretting this decision."

For the first time today, Angie let out a genuine laugh.

"That's what you get for letting me name a kitten I didn't even know we'd have yesterday. I'll come up with something better, right after those cookies are done."

"You really want to do them tonight? I was kind of hoping we could have a quiet evening when the kids are in bed."

"I wish, but not tonight. Maybe after Christmas? We could get a babysitter and go out. Thank you for this." Angie indicated her plate. "I'll just go say hello to Christina, and then we can get started."

"What about dessert?"

"I'll have it later," Angie, already on her feet and on her way out of the kitchen, called.

On the stairs, she could hear the twins sneaking back into the kitchen, followed by their four-legged friends.

What did she say?

She said yes?!

Oooh, awesome!

Angie suppressed a sigh, ignoring that her eyes were welling up from sheer exhaustion. Cats and Christmas trees did not mix. Had anyone considered that?

Chapter Two

NEVA

I t had crossed Neva's mind to try and convince Angie that maybe this year, they could make do with two or three kinds of cookies instead of four. She had left the kitchen for a few minutes only to answer a call from her mother, and when she returned, it was too late. Angie had already put an abundance of ingredients on the counter and started the first batter.

The recipe for the Linzer cookies came from Angie's grandmother, sugar cookies from Neva's side. Cranberry white chocolate was the kids' favorite. The delicious Vegan chocolate cookies had been on the menu since Christina started school. The three girls brought them on the last day of classes, and with those ingredients, no kid was left out.

Good grief, we'll be at this all night.

Neva loved Angie, and she loved Christmas, but she might not share the exact same ambitions for the holiday. Not that she would ever say it out loud. Like Angie, she had a few items on her list she wanted to make time for: Hot chocolate and a movie, visiting the Christmas market, decorating the tree together. That was what it was all about, spending time with family, wasn't it?

Most of their family had retreated to their rooms now. Angie had insisted the process would be more efficient that way.

Neva watched her as she studied a recipe, her reading glasses about to slip off her nose. She was overcome with affection, once more wondering how she could raise the subjects that had been on her mind for weeks now.

Deciding to give it more time, she reached out to brush an imaginary smattering of flour from Angie's cheek.

"You've got a little something there..."

Angie gave her look radiating impatience.

"We don't have time for this. Could you please get started on the chocolate cookies?"

"Of course."

Neva suppressed a sigh. She couldn't blame her wife for not being in a playful mood, given the extent of the task ahead.

"I'll take care of the lights tomorrow morning," Angie continued. She cast an unhappy glance outside the window where the snow was still falling, softly now. They already had four to five inches on the ground. That was another thing they'd have to take care of in the morning, probably before breakfast. Then the kids would be off to school, and Neva would walk the dogs.

"Okay. Are you sure you want to do all of this tonight? We could push some of this to the weekend."

"I don't think we can. We were going to get the guest rooms ready."

"I told you, Mom and Dad will be okay to stay in a hotel overnight."

"It's fine. We have the room, and what if the weather is like this? No, it's better to stick to the plan," Angie decided as she added chocolate chips and cranberries to her batter.

Neva tried to keep up, but she had barely any ingredients in her bowl when Angie started to expertly scoop her batter on the prepared tray and put them in the pre-heated oven.

Neva stared at the table, wondering what she was missing, until it came to her.

"We don't have enough trays."

"What? I thought you bought some more last week."

She was supposed to do it last week, but between homework and housework, her own job, and their usual pre-Christmas shopping trips, it had slipped Neva's mind.

"I forgot. I'm sorry. Usually, we don't do it all in one night."

"Usually, we're not behind like this." Angie sighed. "We'll make do. The dough for the Linzer cookies can just go in the fridge until tomorrow. I'll finish them when I come back from work."

"I can do that," Neva offered, knowing it was futile.

"Thank you, but I'll do it. I'll try to get off work earlier."

"Isn't your colleague still out sick?"

Angie looked surprised that Neva remembered, which she found a bit offensive. Neva let it slide. It had been a long day for all of them, and more long days would follow until she could present her surprise.

The other surprise. She knew Angie was cautious, and perhaps the new kitten hadn't helped, but this was a good one. Neva was proud of herself for keeping the secret this long.

"Yes, she is, but she'll be back on Monday. I might even be able to take a day off."

"That would be great."

"Indeed. There's a lot left to do."

"You know, we have three kids eager to help, especially when it comes to chocolate cookies."

Angie's expression softened some, though her words were a little less encouraging.

"Good. We might need another batch anyway."

Neva decided the best course of action was to just go along for the moment. The sooner they were done, the sooner they could get a good night's sleep and tackle the last few whirlwind days before it was time for some peace.

·♥·♥·♥·♥·♥·

The next morning came quickly. The room was dark except for the light on Angie's nightstand, her side of the bed empty. Neva heard her footsteps on the stairs, and a moment later, she entered the room.

"Hey, you're awake. I found another string of lights in the box, so I changed the ones outside. I also got started on the shoveling. I'll have to leave you the rest. I have to get ready."

"Sure."

Neva hurried to get out of bed so they could share a quick gentle kiss before Angie headed for the shower.

Sounds from Christina's room indicated that the second bathroom would be occupied soon. That left the guest bath, but breakfast wasn't going to make itself. Neva put on a robe and went downstairs where she started the coffee before checking on the non-human babies. Ernie followed her around, wagging his tail, eager for food while Bert was sleeping in the cat bed. The cat...had managed to get into one of the gift boxes they had left on a side table near the tree.

She looked incredibly cute, but Neva knew Angie wouldn't appreciate the state of the box, or the wrapping paper next to it.

"Let's get rid of the evidence, Fluffy, okay?"

She would have to drive by the store and get some more sometime today. When all the furbabies were provided for, she started the coffee and set the table, in time for Fiona and Elsa to arrive. Both of them had their favorite cereal. Christina liked pancakes made in the toaster. Neva put in a couple for her, and one for herself.

Christina was next to arrive. A mumbled "morning" was all they would get out of their eldest until she had some food in her. Angie was last, and she ignored the toast Neva had made for her while drinking her coffee standing up. The hot shower didn't seem to have melted the tension from her shoulders, so Neva got up to step behind her, starting to administer a quick massage.

"That's heavenly, but I don't have time," Angie said, her regret audible. She would love the surprise. Neva was sure of it.

"When you have that day off, we'll make time."

"You have a day off? Can we go to the Christmas market? You said we could go ice-skating this year!" Fiona claimed.

Had they really promised that?

"How about giving Mommy a real day off? We will see the market, but remember we also have a new kitten."

Said kitten was currently curled up in Elsa's lap. Neva caught the soft smile on Angie's face, certain that a few relaxed days would do wonders for all of them. Angie's perfectionism often got the better of her, but she did love the holiday and all that it meant, including their own, specific miracles.

Fifteen years. The twins' birthday. Christina might not believe in Santa Claus anymore, but that didn't hinder the wonder in her eyes. Maybe they didn't quite reach perfection on any given day, but their family was joyful, and this holiday would be no exception.

"That's fine," Angie returned. "We could go on the weekend, right after we prepared the rooms for Grandmas and Grandpas."

Their house would be bursting at the seams. At least their respective parents got along well, and everyone loved the girls, and Bert and Ernie, and they would love Fluffy too. Apparently, the name had stuck for now, and given Angie's ever-expanding lists, she had no time to come up with a new one either.

Neva had big plans, and the previous night of frantic cookie baking was once more confirmation that she was right. Everyone had their comfort rituals, especially around the holidays, but Angie was heading straight for a burnout if she didn't make any changes. Neva was determined to help those changes along. She just had to find the right moment.

"I have to go. Love you all. That includes you, Fluffy." The kitten gave a soft meow as Angie went around the table for goodbye kisses.

After she had left, Neva made sure the girls were dressed and ready for school. Christina took the school bus. Neva, too, got ready and walked Fiona and Elsa to their school, as usual taking Ernie and Bert along for their morning walk.

Once they were back home, she brewed herself another pot of coffee.

She couldn't change much about the upcoming plans. She was lucky to have found a few co-conspirators in Angie's parents, and her own. They would arrive on Christmas Eve as planned to celebrate with them. On Christmas Day...That's where the surprise came in.

She couldn't afford to be daydreaming about it now, because she had to finish shoveling, get some work of her own done and clear the table before picking up Fiona and Elsa.

Last night's baking dishes were still in the dishwasher.

Neva stared at them for a second, wishing she had convinced Angie to stick to two recipes for the night.

One more thing for *her* list. She knew she would have to tread carefully, but she couldn't postpone that conversation forever either.

After taking care of the dishes, she went upstairs to make the bed only to realize Angie had done it earlier. Neva went into the office where she turned on her computer, intent on getting some work done. She had done a few extra hours lately to make up for the time off she had scheduled. Since Angie was out of the house for long hours, she didn't know about Neva's scheming, though it seemed she had noticed something anyway.

Focusing on the task at hand, Neva didn't stop until it was time for another quick walk with the boys.

She learned that due to the updated weather forecast, classes were canceled for the rest of the day and took them back to the house first before she went to pick up Fiona and Elsa. The sidewalks were still slippery, and they were lucky to make it back home without an incident.

She prepared a late lunch while Christina arrived, and they ate together, chatting about their days before it was time for a few more hours of work. Christina's afternoon classes had been canceled as well.

She and Neva emptied another load of dishes and replaced them with those from lunch.

Back in her office, Neva put on some Christmas music and sat down to finish for the day. Something kept nagging at the back of her mind, like she had forgotten an important item. Fluffy had new water, food and litter, and she had claimed her own bed.

Had she promised anything else? Angie had insisted she wanted to finish the baking herself.

"Oh no," Neva said out loud when she remembered the torn box and wrapping paper. Angie would not be amused when she came home and wanted to get a move on the wrapping.

Neva had better take care of this now. She went to the upper floor to knock on Christina's door.

Christina was listening to music on her headphones, definitely not Christmas music, while reading. How she could do the two together, Neva wasn't sure, but growing up in a loud and loving family had to help with multi-tasking.

"Could you watch the twins for a few minutes?" Neva asked. "I have to run an errand quickly."

"Now? It's snowing again."

"I won't be long," Neva promised.

"Sure, okay." She got up to follow her to Fiona and Elsa's room.

"Thank you. You're the best."

Christina gave her a wry smile that was far too adult for Neva's taste. Couldn't they keep the wonder a little bit longer? Regardless of her woes, she had to get going. If she was lucky, she could get started on the wrapping and surprise Angie...again. But from now on, she vowed, they would all be good surprises.

Angie might have been caught off guard by Fluffy, but Neva had seen the way she looked at her. Those eyes had clearly melted her reservations.

Neva shuddered when she stepped outside, despite wearing her warmest coat, scarf, and gloves, but braced herself. Nothing she couldn't handle

Her name meant snow, after all.

Chapter Three

ANGIE

W hen she arrived at work, another colleague was out sick. Angie's hopes of taking time off or even making it to the shopping center during lunch break vanished rapidly. Resigning to her fate, she called Nadine to ask if she could pick up the necklace later, only to get her voicemail.

Angie left a message and texted Neva next: *I'm sorry, but could you finish the cookies? I might be home a little later. Love you.*

Then she settled in front of her computer, though her mind kept wandering. This was the first time they would be hosting both sets of parents at the same time for Christmas. Usually, they visited one of their houses, seldom on the day, because it was also the twins' birthday. Angie and Neva never wanted to make them feel like the occasion was an afterthought.

And the anniversary. Angie had always dreamed of a Christmas wedding, since she was a little girl. Her dream had come true. On a chilly, sunny Christmas Day fifteen years ago, she had married the most amazing, generous, funny, and beautiful woman on the planet, who, by some miracle, loved her back.

It was her lucky day, her lucky season, so why did she feel like everything was about to slip away from her?

"Have you taken a break yet? Here, have some of these."

She looked up to see that Marina had gone on a coffee run. She offered a cup to Angie, together with baked goods that smelled delicious, like cinnamon and clove. Angie's stomach rumbled in response. How much time had passed? She had done her work on autopilot.

"Thank you so much."

"No problem. It's a family favorite."

Angie realized that Marina had brought the treats from home. She winced at the pang of guilt. She had gotten a late start on the Christmas baking, otherwise she would have already brought cookies to the office. Everyone always asked for more.

"Thanks. I'm sorry. I'll bring something tomorrow."

Marina laughed. "We all adore your cookies, but you weren't planning on coming in tomorrow, were you? You know today is Friday?"

"Oh. Right. Monday, then."

"Can't wait."

Marina went back to her own desk, and Angie continued to fill in the form on her screen, almost sighing out loud when she tasted the gingerbread Marina had brought. Perhaps they could try that too or make a gingerbread house with the girls. They had done it with Christina for a few years, when their household consisted of three humans only.

It seemed to her that the harder she tried, the less she was getting done, especially this year. The time was running through her fingers like sand, and it scared her. Soon, Christina would be off to college. The twins would spend more time with their friends.

Neva was so smart and capable. Would she still need her once the kids were off to live their own lives?

Angie shook herself out of her spiraling thoughts and focused on the screen in front of her until Marina returned to her desk.

"I'm so sorry to make you do this, but I have a meeting in a few minutes. Could you get this to the client? I swear, I'll be forever grateful."

She held out an envelope.

"Yes, sure." Angie usually didn't do errands, but she knew that with colleagues being sick, Marina was just as inundated. "I'll come back as soon as possible."

"Thank you so much. I appreciate it."

Angie hurried to her car and got on the road, her progress slower than she would have liked given the amount of work still waiting on her desk.

She passed by an accident site on the other lane, the sight making her shudder. She couldn't see much of the car that seemed to be halfway in a ditch, partly covered in snow already. An ambulance was on the scene.

Angie sent a quick wish that the driver and any passengers would be safe, the sight reminding her to slow down. She hoped their Christmas wasn't completely ruined. She remembered the paperwork following a minor accident she'd had eight years ago. Nobody needed this when their to-do lists were already overflowing.

Angie made it to the client's front desk and delivered the envelope, then drove back to work and continued until Marina arrived with a visitor in tow: Nadine.

"Hi, Angie," she said cheerfully. "I got your message, and I thought I'd just bring it by. I'm so glad you're still here!"

"Thank you, but you didn't have to do that." Angie felt like she had to say it, even though she was beyond relieved. She might have missed Nadine again.

"It's no problem...Except my car broke down a block from here, but that's another story."

"Oh. How will you get home?"

"Don't worry. I'll catch a cab later."

"I'll leave you to it," Marina announced with a knowing smile, and left.

Nadine opened her bag, retrieved a gift box and held it out to Angie.

"I can finally show it to you," she said, beaming with excitement. Inside the box, the necklace lay displayed on a dark blue velvet cloth.

Angie held her breath for several seconds, until the lightheadedness made itself known, and she exhaled.

"It's so beautiful."

It was. Exactly like she had imagined. The two intertwined hearts were dotted with tiny diamonds. Like glistening snow and eternity. She swallowed, her throat tight, unexpected tears prickling behind her eyes. She couldn't wait to give it to Neva. She had also sensed that Neva was distracted lately, and Angie had been scared by what it might mean.

They were okay. They had to be.

She took out her credit card. "You brought the machine, right?"

Nadine shook her head. "I will send you the bill. There's no hurry."

Angie couldn't hold back the frown. She had bought jewelry at this store before. This seemed like a new and strange business practice. Angie didn't like to owe anyone.

"Hang on, I might have enough cash—," she started, reaching for her purse, only to have Nadine interrupt her.

"Please. I insist. And then I'm afraid I must hurry. I have to get a cab before the service shuts down altogether."

Angie cast a quick glance outside the window where the snow was still coming down, thinking that they might have already.

"I'm sorry. Where do you live?" she asked.

"25 Mistletoe Lane. I just moved in a few days ago."

"Really?" What a coincidence. When she and Neva had moved into the neighborhood, they had been amazed by the unique cozy houses, and, she wouldn't deny it, by the name of the street. She remembered Mrs. Gabriel who had abruptly moved out five years ago. The house had been empty since then, though every once in a while, she saw a van from a company to do cleaning, or upkeep outside. "We're neighbors! My wife Neva and I live at 24. You can ride with me."

"Oh, I don't want to impose, but that would be great. I was afraid I might not get that cab after all."

"It's no problem," Angie assured her. "You're just across the street." How had she missed this? And what else had she missed?

She checked her phone, realizing that Neva hadn't answered her question. Trying not to be discouraged, she gave Nadine a smile.

"Come on, let's go. Would you like to have dinner with me and my family?"

"That sounds tempting," Nadine admitted. She waited patiently until Angie had shut down her computer and put on her coat and scarf. Together, they walked to the parking lot. "On the other hand, bringing the jeweler to dinner a few days before Christmas might give you away, and I wouldn't want that to happen."

It was on the tip of her tongue to say that no one in her household would catch the possible implications. Angie held back the statement, fearing it might sound petty.

"It's still over a week until Christmas," she returned. "But it's fine if you have other plans."

"As a matter of fact, I don't. And I have to admit, I'm curious to meet your family. I can tell from the gift you chose that there's a lot of love in your home."

She was right about that. Angie loved everyone in that home with all her heart, but she was so tired. She had to admit she was glad to have a passenger. Talking to Nadine would keep her from falling asleep behind the wheel during the drive home.

Once more, she was driving through heavy snowfall.

Usually, Angie appreciated how everything slowed down around this time of year, time to reflect and anticipate, and get excited about the days to come. Time, especially this year, was a luxury, and she had by far too little of it.

·♥·♥·♥·♥·♥·

Mrs. Gabriel was in her eighties when she lived in the house across the street, but she had decorated her home, including the front yard, each year. Angie and Neva had helped her a few times. Angie had liked her a lot. She, too, was particular about how the lights and ornaments had to be placed. She had a kind word for everyone, and she had exchanged batches of cookies with Angie and Neva. Yet, the only people who came to her house seemed to be the cleaning and landscaping companies.

Angie didn't want to prod, but she had assumed the elderly woman didn't have any family left.

"I wished I had known sooner. She was my friend's great-grandmother," Nadine explained. She leaned back into her seat with a wistful smile, lost in the memory. "When we were little, she hosted the most wonderful Christmas parties. We were allowed to stay up until midnight, but we mostly fell asleep long before...and Santa always delivered. We lost touch when I moved away. I was shocked to find she left me the house, and that there was no one to challenge her will."

"That is quite the story," Angie remarked. "A lot of coincidences had to happen for you to come back here."

"Oh, I wouldn't call it coincidence," Nadine returned with a wink.

Angie wasn't sure what to make of it. As much as she cherished Christmas and its magic, she wasn't naïve and knew that it was created by humans. If you were lucky enough, you could protect and bring some of that childhood joy into your adult years.

"What would you call it?" she asked, genuinely curious.

"Fate, maybe? I have often felt that things happen at the right time. You just have to keep an open mind and read the signs."

Angie kept her eyes on the road, wondering if she was going to regret bringing Nadine to dinner. She tried to relax her tense shoulders without success. All that stress from time issues and last-minute changes was making her judgmental, or maybe she wasn't that good at reading *any* signs.

As she pulled into the driveway, she couldn't believe her eyes. This morning, she hadn't been able to finish shoveling. With the added snowfall today, it looked like no one had done any work today. She parked on the curb, knowing that if she tried to force herself into the parking space, she wouldn't make it out tomorrow.

Neva's car had at least a couple of inches worth of snow on it. Had she gone out earlier for the wrapping paper, or did that mean she had never left? Dejectedly, Angie thought that she might have to cook the dinner she had promised Nadine. She took a deep breath. Tomorrow was Saturday, she realized. No work, but they still had a lot to do for the arrival of their parents.

Still, that antsy feeling wouldn't leave her. She would have to address it later.

"Is everything okay?" Nadine asked, sounding worried.

Was it? Angie wasn't sure. She checked her phone again and found a message from earlier she had missed for some reason.

I'm sorry, I didn't have time. Tonight, I promise.

Angie was about to get out of the car when she realized that the new string of lights she had put on the tree at the break of dawn had gone dark entirely. She didn't think they had another one left to replace this one.

"No, no, no," she said quietly, aware of Nadine's concerned look. "It's not okay. I'm not okay."

Wrapping gifts, preparing the house for guests, taking care of yet another new member of the household—even though she was cute and fluffy and didn't ask for much. Decorating the tree together was another Christmas tradition they couldn't miss. The Christmas market. Ice-skating. All while inside, chaos reigned.

Nothing would get done.

She heard barking and laughter from inside, while no one cared about her mile-long lists, and maybe they were just too nice to tell her.

Did no one care as much as she did?

"Angie?"

She leaned back in her seat and closed her eyes.

"I'm sorry...I just need a moment. Just a second."

In her imagination, she could see it so easily, everyone's joyful faces as they sat around the Christmas tree, music playing in the background, the twins playing quietly with their toys while Christina was engrossed in a book. Her and Neva's parents were watching them with unabashed pride. She and Neva had a moment of quiet and peace, because in her fantasy, Angie had crossed every item off the list, and it was all perfect.

All I wish for every year is a perfect Christmas.

Just once.

Please.

Nadine had to think she had lost her mind, mumbling to herself like this. Angie couldn't help it. The wish had become an almost physical need. She wanted it so much.

Then again, it didn't matter what she wanted. It was just a silly fantasy. She was an adult and had to accept her reality the way it was, accept that she would never live up to that perfect image.

Something would always come up at the last minute, no matter how meticulous her lists were, no matter how early she started writing them.

If only she could just have a break, convince the people she loved that it mattered, all the work they put in year after year.

"Angie? Maybe we should go inside?"

Nadine's worried voice broke the spell, and she opened her eyes to look at her, spooked by the musings that hadn't left her alone all day. She had to get a grip. Only a few days, and their full house would be even fuller.

"Wow, I'm so sorry, I don't usually do this. Yes, let's get inside and have dinner."

Perhaps they should invite Nadine as well this Christmas?

Chapter Four

ANGIE

"*A ngie? Maybe we should go inside?*"

"*Wow, I'm so sorry, I don't usually do this. Yes, let's get inside and have dinner.*"

They finally got out of the car and walked through the ankle-high snow to the front door.

This was what was going to happen: Angie and her family would spend a nice evening with their new neighbor. Everything else, she would deal with another day, because one thing was for sure: There would always be another day, another list, things to do.

This time of year was the most special of all. None of those moments would ever come back, and they had to be planned, scheduled, and executed well.

Angie unlocked the door, momentarily taken aback by the lack of noise, footsteps, and barking that greeted her. In fact, it was eerily silent. Her heart started to beat faster as they stepped into the house.

Where was her family? They were never this quiet. There was always conversation, laughter, and excited barks. Around this time of the year, Christmas music.

"Hello everyone! I'm home! Neva?" Her voice sounded unnaturally loud.

Behind her, Nadine kept a polite distance.

Angie walked further into the house, stopping cold at the sight of the kitchen/living area. This was her home, with all their furniture, plants, and art on the walls, but it didn't look like it.

No clutter, no magazines, no toys—belonging to humans, dogs, or cats—lying around anywhere. Instead of the colorful mix she was used to, the rooms were decorated stylishly for the holidays like out of a magazine, the Christmas tree in the corner shining in colors of silver and gold, matching the rest of the décor. Angie frowned, unable to make sense of what she was seeing. This had to be a dream. She hoped she hadn't fallen asleep while driving home.

Where were the quirky decorations the kids had made over the years? The ornaments she and Neva had bought together, and those they'd brought from their respective childhood homes?

"Neva!"

The urgency in her voice was unmistakable, and to her relief, Neva appeared from upstairs.

"You're home, great! Just in time for dinner."

She approached Angie with an affectionate smile and kissed her gently in greeting. Something was off. Why was she dressed this way? Her perfume was new too. It smelled divine—and expensive.

"Did I miss an anniversary?" she whispered. "Are we going out?"

Neva laughed. "No, and no. Our anniversary is on Christmas Day, remember?"

"I do remember. Did you think of the wrapping paper by any chance?"

"Wrapping paper?" Neva asked, sounding confused.

"Yes, wrapping paper, for the last gifts. Didn't you get my message?"

"What message, Angie? We had them gift-wrapped at the store the other day, remember? Are you okay?" A hint of worry had crept into her tone.

It couldn't be a coincidence that Neva was the second person to ask her that question today.

Angie didn't know how to answer it.

Was she okay? Was she so exhausted that she had imagined sending the message, but never did? That was worrisome indeed, as was this altered environment. They always wrapped gifts together. The kids did it in their rooms, and the results were always adorable.

"I'm fine," she said anyway, "but when did you have the time to do all this?" She hadn't been away that long, and her living room had turned into...she wasn't sure what. Angie didn't dare ask about the decorations. She cast another glance at the tree. It had been just the tiniest bit crooked before, but somehow, even that little imperfection had disappeared.

Behind her, Nadine cleared her throat.

Right. She was being a terrible host on top of it all. Those answers would have to wait.

"Um, I hope you don't mind I brought a guest. Nadine moved into Mrs. Gabriel's house a few days ago."

Come to think of it, Angie hadn't seen any trucks or anything indicating someone had moved in, but she was never home during the day. Strange that Neva had never mentioned it either.

"Oh, that's no problem. We have enough for everyone. You have time to change too. And Nadine, welcome. Would you like a glass of wine to start?"

"Sure. Thank you so much."

Angie stood and stared until Neva, clad in that dress much too formal for a regular Friday evening, turned to her.

"Angie?"

"Change. Yes. Got it. Where are the kids? Bert and Ernie...and the kitten?"

It was Neva's turn to stare, though Angie couldn't understand why.

"Honey, what kitten are you talking about? You're allergic. I would never do that to you, no matter how much the kids beg for one."

Angie let out a sigh in relief. As strange as this was, Neva was still here, and so were the girls.

"Wait. What happened to Fluffy?"

"What do you mean?"

Angie decided the questions had to wait until later. She was hungry and making a fool out of herself in front of a new acquaintance. She caught Nadine's pensive gaze as she said, "Nothing. I'll be quick."

Upstairs in their bedroom, she quickly changed into a top and pants that better matched Neva's outfit, shaking her head at her confused expression in the bathroom mirror. She must have misunderstood something. Maybe they never meant to keep the kitten, just watch her for a few days until they could find a permanent home for her? Angie had to admit she had taken a liking to the tiny bundle, and Bert and Ernie seemed to get along with her too.

Since when did Neva think she was allergic to cats? Spooked, Angie went to Christina's room. Christina wasn't there. She hurried to the twin's room, sighing in relief when she found both of them sitting at their respective desks.

"Girls. Dinner," she said instead of the greeting she had in mind. "Where's Christina?"

Both girls looked at her in confusion.

"What do you mean?"

Had she not been clear enough?

"I mean, why isn't your sister home?"

"Because she's at school?" Elsa and Fiona exchanged a confused look.

That was too much. She left the room and hurried back downstairs to where Neva and Nadine had sat down in the living room, chatting amiably.

"Neva. I need to talk to you, please."

"Of course."

Neva sat her glass on a coaster and got to her feet before she followed Angie into the kitchen, unhurried.

"What's wrong?"

"What's wrong? We seem to be missing a child. And a pet, but Christina is of course priority." Was she losing her mind? Angie felt her face flush with embarrassment when less dramatic possibilities came to mind. "Is she with a friend? I'm sorry if I forgot."

"You've been really stressed lately." Neva reached out a hand and brushed her fingers across Angie's cheek, the tender gesture calming her some. Not enough.

"Are you sure you're okay?" Neva persisted. She touched her palm against Angie's forehead. "You don't have a fever."

"I know I don't have a fever," she said, her impatience returning. "So, where is Christina?"

31

"Still at Caron Academy. She'll be home in a few days, as planned."

She could feel her jaw drop once more. Angie wasn't okay, not even close. On the bright side, Christina was safe. Neva didn't seem to be worried about anything—except Angie's state of mind, but that was another story. How could they even afford Caron?

She and Neva had been stunned when the parents of one of Christina's closest friends enrolled her in the posh boarding school. Aside from financial obstacles, neither of them could ever imagine having their children away for school, at least not before college.

Neva's answer wasn't enough by far, but Angie was nearly dizzy with hunger. They would have to continue this once Nadine had gone home. Unfortunately, she looked quite comfortable on the couch, glass in hand.

If only Angie had known what she'd be walking into...

During dinner, a much more elaborate meal than they usually had on Friday nights, she found no reprieve. It was quiet, too quiet around the table, no one talking.

"So, how was everyone's day?" she asked, hoping her cheery tone didn't sound fake. Even though she was hungry, her stomach was still in knots, making it hard to enjoy the food. She took another sip of her wine, while the twins exchanged curious glances again.

"What did I miss?" she tried again.

"It's all right, go ahead," Neva said softly.

"Go ahead with what?"

"It's fine. Christmas is almost here. We can loosen the rules some, can't we?"

"What rules?" She had trouble not raising her voice.

Nadine smiled. "It was the same at my house when I was little. My parents tried to keep dinnertime quiet, but when the holidays were close, I got too excited."

"Wait. We don't...we never..."

Neva's anxious gaze made Angie halt.

"Since when do we do this quiet dinnertime?"

"Since always?" At this point, Neva sounded almost as panicked as Angie felt.

"Okay." Something was...more than off. Wrong. There was a time when Angie had felt like they had abandoned all rules—everyone talking at the same time, music playing, the dogs demanding attention...She hadn't realized how used she had become to all of it until it disappeared.

"We got an A+ in math," Elsa reported.

"Wow, that's great." Both of them smiled and went back to their plates.

For the first time, Angie noticed the soft music playing in the background. She took a deep breath. She needed to relax more. The quiet she had longed for so often, should help, not hinder. She still wasn't sure what was up with her loved ones, but she made a mental note to let them know she never meant they couldn't talk at all at the dinner table.

Taking in the sights around her, she found the new décor pleasant, if a little cool. Without a doubt, the gold-and-silver tree was pretty, even though she wondered what happened to the ornaments they hung each year. It was nice to change for dinner, use the good plates on a workday.

"Where are the dogs?" she asked.

Nadine, who had been quite talkative earlier, was following the exchange in silence. Angie could tell she was curious. She would be, too, in her place.

"Honey, we have one dog, and he knows he's not allowed in the room when we eat."

To Neva's credit, she spoke quietly, though in the surrounding silence everyone could still overhear her words.

Should she have a guilty conscience for sometimes feeling like it had all been too much? Angie had many questions, but she figured if no one was upset, perhaps she shouldn't be either? She glanced at the packages under the tree, perfectly wrapped in silver and gold. Everything was so unfamiliar. New didn't have to mean bad, did it?

She couldn't shake the confusion. Maybe she was still dreaming, a long, weird, and much too elaborate dream. She needed a good night's sleep.

In the morning, she and Neva would laugh about it, the idea that no one was talking at the table, that Christina attended Caron, that they only had one dog who wasn't allowed to sleep under the dining table. So strange.

Just like Neva dressing up and producing a four-course dinner.

The wine was excellent, and the raspberry mousse cake and coffee the perfect ending to a scrumptious meal. Finally, she allowed herself to taste something, now that it was almost over, and that was part of the problem too.

Everyone was safe. Christmas was around the corner, and Nadine had created the most beautiful gift for Neva. What did she have to worry about? She was savoring the last spoonful when Nadine said,

"Thank you so much for having me tonight, but I should really go. It's late."

"It's Friday," Neva said. "Don't you want to stay for a nightcap?"

"Thank you, maybe another time?"

"I'll walk you out." Angie got to her feet as well. "Thank you again for your wonderful work," she addressed Nadine when they had reached the front door.

Nadine leaned against the closed door, smiling.

"It was my pleasure, Angie. How do you like it?"

"Like what?" Angie asked, confusion returning.

"Your wish."

"My..."

"Your perfect Christmas."

She still wasn't sure what Nadine was talking about, though her unease grew with each word.

"It's peaceful and quiet, isn't it? All that chatter, barking, singing, you could never concentrate and cross everything off the list. Three kids at once, three pets, it's a lot to handle."

"What are you talking about? We still have three kids...one pet, apparently. Wait, how did you know?"

"What do you think?" Her tone was patient, and a tad patronizing, Angie thought. "I made it come true for you. You're not confused, Angie. This is your wish, and it came true just before Christmas. You're welcome."

Nadine left before Angie could react. When she yanked the door open again, Nadine was gone.

No.

None of this was possible.

Christina didn't go to Caron. The twins were never quiet, and they had three beloved pets, and they didn't do formal Fridays. Angie hurried back into the living room, the soft music now getting on her nerves. What had happened to this place? Was someone playing a prank on her because she had insisted everyone go along with her lists?

This wasn't what she had wished for!

In the kitchen, she opened the fridge, expecting to see the last batch of dough she had prepared the day before. It wasn't there.

"Neva!"

"Right here, darling." Neva sounded like she was close to tears. What was she keeping from Angie? "What's wrong?"

"Where's the dough?"

"What dough?"

"Yesterday's cookie dough! You said you didn't have the time to finish up."

Neva laid a hand on her shoulder and turned her around.

"Angie, please, stop. You know we haven't had the time to bake cookies in years."

"What is happening?"

"Please, take a breath and sit down. You're scaring me. Should we call the doctor?"

"I don't need a doctor. I need to know what happened here. Where is Christina?"

"I told you. At Caron. She'll be here next Thursday."

Angie closed the door of the fridge with more vehemence than necessary, making bottles and glass jars rattle.

"Christina doesn't go to Caron. Where is she, and what happened to the pets?"

"We can call Christina right now if you want," Neva suggested, sounding anxious.

"Yes, I want to."

"Okay." Neva took out her cell phone and opened a video chat. After three rings, a sleepy Christina appeared on the screen.

"Hi Moms. Everything okay?"

"Yes, of course. Angie was home late and wanted to see you. We miss you."

"Miss you too, but I'll be home soon." Christina yawned. "I'm sorry, but I have a test tomorrow."

"That's okay," Angie reassured her. "I'm sorry. Good night, sweetie."

"Good night, Moms."

"Come with me." Neva took Angie's hand and pulled her along back past the living room to another sitting area. A sunroom? They had talked about turning a storage room into one but never gotten around to do it. Now, everything was clean and in order, and in his dog bed, Bert stood up, wagging his tail.

"Come on, Brad. Say hi to Angie."

Brad? *Who names a dog Brad?* And why was everyone so weirdly polite? Even the *dog*? She still wasn't ruling out an elaborate prank or strange dreams from complete exhaustion.

Tomorrow. Tomorrow would be better.

"You're okay now?" Neva asked, her hand gentle on Angie's back. Brad followed them into the living room but stayed at a distance from the tree and gifts.

"I think so." About to sit down, she froze. "When did we get that piano?"

Chapter Five

NEVA

With their household well on track for the holidays, this hadn't been the evening Neva had expected. To her relief, Angie seemed back to her old self the next morning when they had breakfast together before the twins woke up, going over the to-do list for the day.

Speaking to Christina had apparently helped her, and Angie didn't mention the mysterious missing pets any longer.

Neva thought back to how long it had taken them to decide to get Brad...never mind two of them, and a kitten. With a couple of colleagues on her project out sick, Angie had taken on a lot more work. She clearly hadn't gotten enough sleep or rest, and Neva was determined to make up for it.

Baking cookies? She shook her head at the thought. Why go to the trouble when you could just buy a delicious bag at the bakery? They had decided early on to be careful with sweets around the kids. Christmas was an exception, sure, but they still didn't want to overdo it.

Angie was going over her lists, looking both surprised and delighted that there was nothing left to do.

"When did we get all of this done?" she asked, meeting Neva's gaze with a smile. "This is good. Now we only have to get the rooms ready for our parents."

The relief she'd felt since waking up this morning was about to vanish again.

"What do you mean, love?"

"They're still coming for Christmas, right? To celebrate our anniversary and the girls' birthdays with us? Not to mention, Christmas?"

"Where did you get that idea? We'll do lunch with your parents on Christmas Eve as usual. Why did you think my parents would come? It's just too far. We said we might try for Spring Break next year, remember?"

At this point, Neva wasn't sure what Angie remembered. She didn't want to be impatient with her wife, especially not now, but how had she come up with that elaborate story? Angie was too kind, and too much into her perfect Christmas to joke around with any of it. Neva couldn't help feeling melancholic. She hadn't seen her parents in months, and the girls were growing up so fast. It would be nice to have everyone over sometime.

"Spring Break," Angie repeated. She took a sip of coffee, winced, and got up to refill both their cups. "Okay. And we do this every year on Christmas Eve."

Since she had returned from work last night, almost every sentence directed at Neva had been a question. This time, her voice went up only a tiny bit, as if she was resigning to her fate.

"We do. The five of us go out for brunch on Christmas Day and have a quiet holiday while the kids are off from school. Just like we always dreamed. Right?" It was starting to feel like she was the one whose story didn't make sense, her tone bordering on desperate. Beyond bizarre, having to explain their familiar routines.

But whatever happened to Angie, they would be able to fix it. Because they could fix everything if they stuck together and always told each other the truth. At least it was what had made them get through many challenges, and into this beautiful home with their family. It was what they instilled in their children.

"Right," Angie said though she didn't sound convinced. "These are all done," she said with regard to the lists. "What is the plan for today?"

"I checked with the babysitter, and they're free tonight. We could go out, and maybe see a movie?"

"Yes. That would be nice."

Once again, Angie picked up the sheets of paper filled with items in her immaculate handwriting.

"I can't believe...When did we have the time?" she wondered out loud, again.

"Your time management is excellent. That is why. And I hear someone else is ready for breakfast."

Neva got up to put the twins' breakfast on the table. She wasn't sure what to make of the surprise in Angie's expression, though no comment followed. Elsa and Fiona walked in, all smiles, and took their seats at the table.

"Hey. Mandy is coming for your piano lessons today. Are you excited?"

"Yay!" they echoed.

Angie choked on her sip of coffee.

· ♥ · ♥ · ♥ · ♥ · ♥

Later, she caught Angie listening in awe as the twins practiced *We wish you a Merry Christmas* with Mandy. The woman had her work cut out for her, but she was good with children, and Neva had to admit they had made a lot of progress since the beginning.

They wanted to give them as many options as possible, even if it required a lot of crunching numbers and overtime work. Neva was lucky to be able to work from home, so she could watch the twins. They were starting to ask a lot of questions about Caron, but in Neva's opinion, it was too early for them. Having Christina away for the semester was still hard.

She frowned as she remembered Angie's bizarre reaction the other night.

Had she really forgotten that their daughter was in boarding school? Everyone had reassured them...To be on the safe side, she would make sure Angie saw their family doctor after all. Before Christmas, so they could all enjoy the holidays without worrying.

Angie had become aware of Neva's scrutiny and came over to her. Up close, she looked more troubled than Neva would have liked.

"I know they're not quite there yet, but I promise, they will get better."

"That's not it. If they are never great at it, but enjoy it, we'll be okay. They know that, right?"

"Of course, they do. What kind of question is that?"

Angie didn't elaborate.

"I don't think I feel like a movie tonight. Would it be okay if we just went to dinner later?"

"I don't mind. Whatever you prefer." She didn't want to sound like a broken record, but she had reason for concern, didn't she?

"Thank you. By the way, what did you think of Nadine?"

The question caught her off guard.

"I...I don't know, why? She seems nice. And if Mrs. Gabriel gave her the house, she must be."

"Yeah." Angie seemed to be far away.

"In any case, you must have talked to her more than I have." Neva had seen her move into the house the previous week, and she knew the jewelry store Nadine ran in the small shopping center close by. They hardly went though, too many crowds for Angie.

"Maybe. There was something she said...Never mind. What else is on the agenda for today?"

"I have a bit of work left, after that, perhaps a walk with Brad, and then we get ready for dinner?"

"Sounds nice," Angie said, though the wistful tone of her voice didn't quite fit. What was going on? "Why don't you go finish up, and I'll find something to wear for dinner?"

"I'll do that."

Neva was even more worried when she came back downstairs an hour later and couldn't find Angie. She didn't want to scare Fiona and Elsa who had finished their lesson and were playing in their room.

She didn't want to leave them alone either.

Before she could talk herself into a full-blown panic, she saw Angie through the window, striding purposefully towards their neighbor's house. In equal parts curious and concerned, Neva remained behind the window and watched her ring the doorbell and wait. Nothing happened. Angie rang again, her posture radiating impatience. She knocked on the door. Neva winced when she realized Angie wasn't wearing gloves. After a few more minutes and a couple of more attempts later, she turned around.

Neva retreated from the window so it wouldn't look like she was spying on her, which was exactly what she was doing.

Angie returned to the house with an expression of frustration and resignation. Neva waited a few heartbeats before she met her in the hallway.

"Where did you go?"

"Just outside, getting a bit of fresh air." Angie shrugged. "Is there anything you need?"

Yes. I need you to be all right. Neva stepped forward and embraced her.

"Nothing in particular. I missed you."

She expected Angie to laugh, after all she'd been only a few footsteps away, but instead she remained tense in Neva's arms.

"I know the feeling," she said. "It's nice outside though. Let's go walk Bert...Brad."

"Yes, let's do that. I'll get the twins."

After spending almost an hour in the winter wonderland created by three days of almost constant snowfall, Neva could almost convince herself that everything was back to normal.

Brad enjoyed the snow, making the twins laugh. They admired the decorations in the neighborhood. Nothing was too overdone or weird, everything tasteful and cozy. Just like they liked it.

"I know it's close to dinner, but how about a hot chocolate for everyone?" Angie suggested, startling her.

What was it with all these new habits? Maybe they were old habits, but they had to stick to the plan, didn't they?

"We could do it tomorrow," Neva suggested. "This close to dinner we'll just spoil our appetites."

"Sure." Angie looked more disappointed than the girls who kept walking between them. "Tomorrow."

She had never mentioned why she had gone over to Nadine's.

Chapter Six

ANGIE

She had resigned to the fact that it was better to wait with any more confrontations until she could talk to Nadine. Truth be told, Angie wasn't sure what to tell—or ask—her, but her life had changed overnight, and as unrealistic as it was, Nadine seemed to have some idea why.

Okay, the next time she wouldn't sneak away or pound on her front door. She would stay calm. Have a reasonable conversation with her neighbor, because there had to be a reasonable explanation for her reality, and why it differed so dramatically from the one she remembered.

In which there were toys and books all over the place, and everyone was always talking and laughing. While they were paying attention to what they ate, no one had ever argued against that one extra snack around Christmas.

Everyone in her home seemed so...polite and reserved. Christina wasn't home. That was the strangest occurrence, but everything else was disconcerting on various levels. Bert—Brad.

And no one could or wanted to tell her how all of it had come to pass...

As she changed into different clothes for the restaurant, she was aware of Neva's concerned gaze on her. Not to worry her any more, and also to buy time for herself, Angie had decided to play along for now.

"Are you sure you'll be okay to go out tonight? You seemed really upset earlier."

That's because I am.

"I'm fine," she said, forcing a smile. "I think I got a little stressed with the holidays so close."

"Yes." Neva sat next to her on the bed, laying an arm around her shoulders. "To think that Christmas Eve is only a week away."

Angie all but jumped to her feet.

"Wait, what? A week?"

"But everything is ready. We have reservations for the restaurant, Chris will be home soon, and...Angie?"

"No, it's okay." She couldn't draw any more attention to herself. One week! That meant she had somehow lost three days? How was that possible, and if it happened, why did Neva act like she knew nothing about it? "You're right, we're ready." Angie had no idea anymore if that was true. "I'm hungry too. Let's go?"

She could tell Neva wasn't entirely convinced.

"Please. I'm sorry—and I'm starving. Let's say goodnight to the girls and go."

She had a moment of anxiety entering the girls' room, but to her relief, Billie, the babysitter, was the same sixteen-year-old Angie remembered. She lived at the end of the street and had babysat the twins for a couple of years.

"You have a good night," she said and kissed both Fiona and Elsa. "Billie, thank you for making time."

"Of course, Ms. Winters."

She was quiet and reliable, and the girls loved her. It would be fine. Everything would be fine.

·▾·▾·♥·▾·▾·

They took a cab, and Neva gave instructions to the driver.

"Gourmet French cuisine? Can we afford that?" Angie was only half joking. When they went out, it was usually to the family-run diner in town, or on rare occasions, to *La Dolce Vita* over in Chestnut Hill. She was certain they had never been to this one since it opened five years ago.

Neva gave her a strange look.

"Never mind. I can't wait."

She felt a bit intimidated when the hostess saw them to their table upon their arrival. Angie couldn't remember when they had last dined in a place with white tablecloths and wondered if they were underdressed.

"Not to be annoying, but this isn't cheap. Is there an occasion I'm not aware of?"

Neva's smile held a hint of wistfulness.

"The company had record profits, and you know they gave me a nice bonus this year. I think I can afford to take out my wife for one nice dinner."

Record profits? Bonus? Since when did Neva work for a company? Maybe she had done some freelance work for them?

"I'm not complaining. This is beautiful." It was. A huge, decorated tree stood at the far end of the room, and every table had a Christmas themed centerpiece. To her relief, the waitress arrived with their menus, and they spent a few minutes on choosing wine and food. She probably needed food more, but the first sip of wine helped calm her mind some.

Neva, too, seemed more relaxed. Angie wasn't going to spoil the moment by asking what firm, and what bonus. Come to think of it, she had seen none of Neva's painting supplies in the house.

The house...She needed to take a look around on her own, see what else had changed.

The *Coq au Vin* and red wine were definitely real. Every bite tasted delicious.

While they enjoyed their meal, Angie tried to sum up her situation. They were still going to celebrate Christmas as a family. That was what mattered, right? She had to know if Christina was happy in her school, and she had to get a hold of her own parents. It was so strange to think that they'd only have lunch together. Angie knew that they, like Neva's parents, loved spoiling the girls senseless every year. What had changed?

"You're far away," Neva observed, taking her hand.

"I'm fine, just looking forward to Christmas, and having Christina home." It wasn't a lie, even though there was a whole lot more on her mind.

Angie's gaze went past Neva to a server who was taking the order of an older couple, her jaw dropping when she recognized the woman.

How was that possible...?!

Scratch that, apparently, she had been catapulted into an alternate universe where nothing was impossible. Yeah, right. She retracted her hand and got up.

"Excuse me for a moment? I'm good," she hurried to say. "I just want to say hi to someone."

She had to hurry to catch up with the woman who returned to the kitchen in quick strides.

"Nadine! Wait! Please, I need to talk to you."

The woman turned to her with a smile. Angie had almost hoped that she was mistaken, but it was definitely Nadine, and they were both standing in the kitchen of the restaurant, the staff watching them with curious gazes.

"Angie, hello. What a coincidence."

"Could we go somewhere else? Just for a moment?"

"Sure."

Nadine led her past her working colleagues, line cooks and other servers, to a dimly lit hallway. At this moment, Angie wasn't sure if she could trust her neighbor, but she needed answers. That was priority.

"What would you like to know?"

"About my wish," she began, realizing what she was about to say would sound completely bizarre to any reasonable person. It sounded bizarre to her, and she was living it! She had to take the risk.

"Are you enjoying it?" Nadine asked, beaming. "Isn't it great? A week before Christmas, and you don't have to worry about a thing. No elaborate dinners or preparations, no dishes, just a few quiet days with your family. And you and Neva have finally more space and money to spend."

"What are you talking about? Wait, why are we talking about this? What did you do?"

"Not much," Nadine declared with a shrug. "You made the wish. I did the rest."

"How?" Her frustration and anxiety were rising again. "Who are you?"

Nadine wasn't fazed by the confrontation. In fact, she acted like she was used to it.

Am I losing my mind?

"You could say I'm a wish granter. Every Christmas, I give people the chance to get the lives they want."

"But this isn't what I want," Angie replied without hesitation. Never mind bizarre, she had to make her point clear. "Neva doesn't seem to be happy. Our child is in boarding school, whose idea was that? Wait, Ernie and Fluffy didn't end up in a shelter, did they?"

"No," Nadine said patiently. "In this reality, they never existed."

"*This* reality?" Her voice had crept up a notch, again. "What else is there? No, don't answer that. Tell me how I can fix it!"

"I already fixed what you thought was wrong. The rest is for you to figure out."

"But I don't know what to do!" This couldn't be happening. "If you did this, you can reverse it, can't you?" Did she sound insane? It sounded insane to her, but here she was in the hallway of a French restaurant, imploring a woman she barely knew to undo her Christmas wish. "I never meant...any of that. Okay, perhaps I didn't make it so clear, but I didn't want everything to change! I just wanted a moment to rest!"

"Then you'll probably be fine."

Angie had spun around, about to go back to her table, but something in Nadine's tone stopped her. "Probably? What do you mean?"

"Well, I can't tell you what to do." Nadine sounded far too calm and patient for the content of this conversation. "But you must find out before midnight on Christmas Eve."

"What happens if I don't?"

She couldn't believe it. Angie didn't want to say it out loud. Nadine had no such reservations.

"Then everything will stay as it is."

"No."

"That is the way it goes. Good luck, Angie. I'm afraid I must go back to work." Just like that, she was gone.

Angie stood for almost a minute, her thoughts racing, before she went back to the table.

"Are you all right?" Neva asked.

She wasn't, but she was getting tired of that question.

"You look like you've seen a ghost."

"It's okay. I thought I recognized someone, but I was mistaken."

"Okay." There was a hint of disappointment to Neva's tone. "Would you like a dessert?"

How was she ever going to approach this with her? She couldn't, Angie realized. Neva, in this reality, as bizarre as that sounded, had no idea. She would be as clueless as Angie was, and even more worried.

"I would. That chocolate hazelnut mousse sounds amazing," she said, smiling, while wondering how she was going to get them back to normal.

Before Christmas, even.

Easy.

·♥·♥·♥·♥·♥·

Long after Neva had fallen asleep next to her, Angie lay awake, formulating a plan. She had to push aside her disbelief and then approach the situation rationally. If she had done something to land in this reality, she had to be able to undo it.

There had to be some sort of lesson in it. She was smart, she was determined, she was going to make it.

Wasn't she?

She reflected back on her interactions with all of her loved ones in the past weeks. Sure, she might have been a bit curter and more demanding recently, but all of it happened because she had so much work to do. Covering her own and her colleagues' workload at the office, then coming home to make sure all items would be crossed off the never-ending Christmas list.

That had to be it!

Work. She had given her job so much time lately and not even tried to take one day off. She could redeem that, right at the start of the week. Angie still couldn't fathom how she had been transported to this place that wasn't quite her life, but she would do what she could to bring them home. All she had to do was to make more time to actually be home, and the rest would follow.

Whatever ghost had come to visit her, she would solve the riddle and give her family the best holiday they could imagine, the same way she had done it for years. Just better.

Chapter Seven

NEVA

After Angie had jumped up from her chair to run after some person she might or might not know and didn't return for minutes, Neva formed a decision. She called in a favor, and Monday morning, they sat together in the waiting room of Dr. McEwen's practice.

Angie didn't look happy, but Neva had not seen an alternative. The twins were at school, and she would have time to stay until she had to pick them up, and Angie would go to her job.

"I'm sorry," she whispered, even though they were alone in the room. "I think this is important."

Angie gave her a faint smile. "It's okay. I might have overdone it in the last few weeks. I'll follow doctor's orders, whatever they are. I want us to enjoy the holidays."

Neva wanted to say something, but the doctor arrived to greet them.

"Good morning. How are you?"

"Great," they almost said in unison.

"That's good to hear." Ignoring the awkward moment, Dr. McEwen, "Dr. Holly," as her youngest patients, including the twins, called her affectionately, showed nothing but warmth and compassion. They'd been with her since she had opened her practice, and they could trust her.

Neva could breathe a little easier.

"Angie, you can come with me."

When she was alone, Neva pulled out her tablet to do some work, but she couldn't concentrate. How was it that Angie couldn't seem to remember a big part of their lives...Worse, she had apparently imagined a whole other life? Was she miserable? Were they? Or was this about something even worse?

They had made compromises, sure, but only to give their children the best possible opportunities, and for themselves, to benefit from their hard work. They had made those decisions early on, to make their careers fit their family lives.

It scared Neva that it might all fall apart. She wished they could fast forward to Christmas, past the lunch, straight to the nice quiet Christmas Day evening that Angie loved so much. She couldn't lose her.

Instead of getting anything done, she worked herself in a state of near panic with worst case scenarios, until Angie returned, looking pensive, though not scared or shocked. That had to be a good sign.

Neva jumped to her feet and pulled her close.

"What did she say?"

Angie shrugged but made no move to get out of her embrace. "We'll have to wait for the blood test, but it looks like there's nothing wrong with me." She gave a wry laugh. "She asked about stress. What can I say? It's that time of the year, right?"

Neva wasn't sure what to answer to that. Getting stressed out of one's mind was not the point of Advent.

"I still have time to drive you to work," she offered eventually.

"That would be nice. Let's go get a coffee somewhere first. There are some things we should talk about."

"But you said..."

Angie stepped back, making a dismissive gesture.

"Not about me. About next year."

That didn't feel reassuring either.

They found themselves a small café that offered a variety of breakfasts. Angie went with a pastry.

Neva wasn't that hungry, but she had toast with coffee.

"I want to make some changes," Angie declared once a server had brought their orders. "All this overtime, it doesn't add up to a lot. I'll talk to Marina later."

Not that Neva minded Angie taking it easy, especially now, though the announcement surprised her.

"You're sure you'll be okay with that? You love that job."

"I love you and the kids more. And we could have your and my parents over for dinner this Christmas."

Neva nearly dropped her knife. The doctor might not have found anything, but Neva knew something was off if Angie wanted a full house for Christmas.

"But...That's on short notice. And you know my parents live too far away to just drop by."

"That's all right. We have a guest room, and a few more days to prepare. Everything else is done for the holidays."

"I suppose I could ask them. They were going to my sister's for Christmas Eve, but they might come over for Christmas Day if the weather allows."

"It's supposed to be sunny, no snow. Call them."

"Now?"

Angie laughed, and the sound made her hopeful and happy, even if the context was still off.

"I think you can wait until you're home. I'm sure they'd like to see the girls, right? And something else, what were we thinking sending Christina off to Caron? Let's talk to her about transferring, at the latest once the schoolyear is finished, but perhaps we can do it before Spring Break."

"We can't do that!" Angie's face fell, and Neva wasn't sure whether to hug her again, or shake her. They hadn't taken this decision lightly. There had been tears, and serious decisions to be made regarding the financing of their venture. "Christina is happy at Caron. She's thriving, and all her friends are there. Why would we take her out now?"

Her tone might have been a bit harsh, but she'd been living in constant worry since Angie started acting so strange. Come to think of it, this had started when she invited the jeweler, Nadine, to dinner. There was another explanation Neva couldn't bring herself to think of. No. Angie would never do such a thing.

"I'm sorry. It's just...I miss her."

"I understand. I miss her too, but this is good for her. She's been coming into her own, her grades are phenomenal, and she has good friends."

Neva, too, would have loved to have her closer, but it wasn't always about what *they* wanted, was it?

"Can we just sit down and talk about this? With her? If she really does want to stay..." Angie took a deep breath. "Then, okay, she'll stay. I just want to be sure she's happy. That all of you are."

"She is. We are. I promise you." *Are you?* "I'll call Mom and Dad after I pick up Fiona and Elsa."

"Yes, please. We'll have a great Christmas, and please, stop worrying. Dr. McEwen is pretty sure they aren't going to find anything in that blood test. I just need to cut down on work a bit, and perhaps you should too."

People could change their mind, Neva reasoned. She didn't know Angie harbored so many doubts about Caron, or the way they did things in their day-to-day life.

They would have to make time to talk, beyond the holiday schedule. As far as that was concerned, she thought they had made good progress. Her parents would be thrilled to see their grandchildren. She, too, was thrilled, and perhaps a house full of joy and laughter was exactly what she and Angie needed.

As long as they were both still in this, they would manage.

She had to believe it.

Chapter Eight

ANGIE

She was making progress. A few more days, and everything would right itself. She had figured it out. While she would have preferred to have a clearer decision regarding Christina and Caron, it was a good first step.

Neva would hopefully relax now that she knew Angie's unusual behavior—unusual to Neva, at least—didn't have any physical reasons.

Neva. Angie marveled at the fact that she, and the girls, were the same familiar people she loved most in the world, even if that world had changed without warning. She would hold on to that, as long as she still had to maneuver this strange reality.

Marina, her boss, had to deal with unusual Angie as well, and she was more understanding than Angie had hoped.

"My doctor tells me I should do more to avoid stress. I'm afraid she's right. I've been doing the job of several people for the past few weeks, and I can't continue like this. I'm going to need a few days off. My preference would be two days before Christmas, and two days after, but I can be a little flexible."

She realized she was running out of breath and stopped before she would make herself lightheaded.

Marina regarded her with what Angie could only describe as a neutral expression.

"Angie, of course. I was wondering if you'd ever ask. Marley will be back tomorrow."

"Really?"

"It's no problem. I don't want any of you to burn yourself out, especially before Christmas."

"Okay, then...Thank you."

"Is there anything else?" Marina asked when she hesitated.

"No. Again. Thank you. I appreciate this very much."

She returned to her desk both triumphant and a little perplexed. Who would have known it was this easy?

If the lesson she had to learn was to make more time for her family, she had succeeded. Whether she had been living a strange dream or a hallucination, or actual, unbelievable, magic—whatever it was, it would be reversed now that she had figured out the reason for it. And even though she had talked about a quiet Christmas, having everyone over for dinner would make it even better. They'd have a great time.

As the end of her shift neared, she couldn't help getting excited. She would come home to a reality she knew, with all of her children home, and everyone telling stories about their day at dinner. With a few days off, she'd be better equipped to do last minute preparations, and this strange time, and the time lost...They never had to talk about it again. She had fixed it. After all, that's what Angie did.

· ♥ · ♥ · ♥ · ♥ · ♥ ·

There were no lights on the tree outside. Maybe the string was beyond repair, and Neva had removed it. Angie parked her car and all but ran to the front door, eager to see the fruits of her problem-solving labor.

The house was dark, but she found a note by the door.

Called Mom and Dad, they said yes! Brought Fiona and Elsa to their tutor, and I'll wait with them. Billie took Brad for a walk. Love, N.

Tutor? Since when...

Angie went around the house, turning on lights, her heart sinking with disappointment and disbelief when she realized nothing had changed. The living room still looked the same, shiny, expensive-looking decorations, not a throw pillow out of place, no books or toys lying around. Upstairs, Christina's bed was immaculately made.

They still had a sitting room instead of Neva's workshop.

Why hadn't her actions changed anything?

Angie had no idea who that tutor was, or how long Neva and the twins would be out, but she couldn't wait. She hurried back to her car and drove all the way to the shopping center, not stopping until she had reached Nadine's store.

Nadine was behind the counter, working on a piece of gold jewelry.

Angie halted. Had she really seen her work as a server at the restaurant last Saturday night? Had she imagined that entire conversation? No.

Nadine looked up with a smile when she heard the bell over the door.

"Angie, good evening. What can I do for you?"

"You know—" She stopped herself short of using a swear word. "Why is this still going on? I did ask for a few days off to spend more time with my family. I get it. I got so caught up in work and getting everything done perfectly and in time...You need to help me!"

Nadine studied her, her gaze open and patient.

Angie didn't have the same patience.

"Please!"

"I told you, I'm sorry, but it's not up to me."

"You must know something! Don't you have, I don't know, a general idea about how to undo a curse?"

"It's not a curse, Angie," Nadine said softly. "I do understand that it's something people feel sometimes when their wish comes true."

"Everyone is so distant and polite, like we're not even a family. I..." She shook her head, laughing at the absurdity though she felt more like crying. "I still don't know what happened to our pets. Neva loved painting in her studio, and now it's a sitting room with a dog bed. And what's that about us going over to my parents' for lunch? We have a whole house."

"If you feel like the solution is there, maybe you should give it a try." Nadine went back to her meticulous work.

"Does that mean this is it? I was obsessing too much over the parents' visit? I told Neva to call hers, and that we would get the guest rooms ready. Do I have to work harder to convince Neva to have Christina change schools?"

Nadine straightened and met her gaze once more.

"Like I said, none of it is up to me, but I sense that your wish is interacting with those of others."

"What does that even mean?"

"They might have their own opinions."

"Yeah." Angie sighed, frustrated with the lack of answers. Did Nadine really not have them? Was she lying? Days before Christmas? Who did that? "What do I do now?"

"You keep trying," Nadine encouraged her. "Not all is lost. You still have time."

"I guess you're right. Thank you."

"You're welcome."

Angie walked out of the store, none the wiser. It was getting late, but she couldn't bring herself to leave the shopping center yet.

A line of kids was still waiting to meet Santa. A little girl chatting excitedly to her mother caught her eye.

She looked a lot like Christina at that age. Angie recalled the incredible joy, all the plans and promises when they brought her home. Was it possible that Neva was right, and she loved being at Caron? Why couldn't she remember anything about it? Had she been at work most of the time while Neva was left to make those decisions? Why hadn't she said anything?

How on earth are we making enough money to send her to Caron?

The questions didn't end. Angie walked past Santa's workshop and into a candy store. She felt the need to treat her loved ones, and herself.

Maybe some sugar would do the trick and help her get to the bottom of this.

Chapter Nine

ANGIE

So, there was something else she had to figure out. Angie was good at figuring things out. She was good at planning and scheduling, and this would help her solve whatever riddle she was looking at.

Maybe the universe didn't consider taking a few days off a big enough gesture. She had to do some investigating. The next day on her lunch break, she sent a text to her parents.

I'll call you later, but I wanted to ask if you'd like to come over for dinner on Christmas Day. Neva's parents will be there too.

Next, she called Christina. When she didn't pick up right away, Angie tried another couple of times and got worried. Her next call went to Caron. Magically, the principal's number was saved in her cell phone.

"I can't reach my daughter," she said without preamble. "I need to speak to her."

"Ms. Winters. I have Christina right here."

"Mom," her daughter whined a moment later. "We are not allowed to pick up the phone in class. I got called into the principal's office."

"I'm sorry, baby..." She halted, and for a few seconds it felt like everyone, including the principal, was holding their breaths.

"Why are you calling me? Is something wrong?" Christina now sounded alarmed. "Are Mama and the twins okay?"

"Yes, we're fine. I'm sorry," she said again. "Can you speak?"

"What does that mean?"

"Chrissie, I need to ask you something. Do you want to come home?"

"Mom? You are freaking me out. You know I'm coming home in a few days."

"Yes." Angie took a deep, hopefully calming, breath. "I mean, for good. If you're not happy there, you could always come back and go to school here. Whatever you want."

"I'm good. I need to go back to class," Christina returned. "And I'm meeting Hayley and Ash later. We want to go Christmas shopping."

So, they had fewer pets now, but their kids had friends and piano teachers and tutors Angie had never heard about. She fought back the rising panic.

"That sounds really nice. I'm sorry I interrupted your class. I'll see you next week. Love you."

"Love you too, Mom."

That was the most reassuring thing she had heard in a while. If the lesson was to bring Christina home for good, well, she would have to work harder on that. She glanced at the new message notification on her screen and opened it to realize it was from her parents.

Honey, we thought you had reservations for Christmas Day as usual. I'm sorry, but Dad and I booked a trip. We are leaving very early on Christmas Morning.

That wasn't going to work out either. Would she get points for trying, at least? How could she know if she was on the right track?

Angie finished her workday, antsy and unsure what to do next. When she came home, Neva was still working, and the girls were playing in their room.

It was so quiet, her unease kept growing by the minute. She brewed another coffee and opened the pantry to take out some of the chocolate she had bought the day before, when it came to her. Store-bought cookies for Christmas? She wasn't going to have that.

Angie found a channel that played Christmas music and started taking out ingredients, including the Vegan chocolate chips, and spread them out on the counter. She could have one, maybe two batches in the oven before dinner.

The familiar task finally helped calm her, though she might not be as quick and efficient in her new reality as she had thought: She was halfway through cutting out the first batch when Neva arrived, stopping cold at the sight.

"Hey. I thought at least two kinds would be nice."

"But..."

Something about her tone made Angie look up. Neva looked flabbergasted.

"It's still early."

"It's...We still have to make dinner. I thought you didn't like messes."

Angie glanced at the island's countertop. To her, it looked fine, though a bit of flour was all over the place. She was just about to cut out another set of sugar cookies.

"This isn't...never mind. I'll clean up before dinner, I promise."

"No, that's fine. Can I help?"

Right track, again?

Time would tell.

She handed Neva a couple of cookie cutters, a heart and a tree, their fingers touching when Neva took them. "If you could cut out a few more of these…"

They worked together for a few minutes, and Angie put a sheet of cookies in the oven. When she turned back to Neva, she was struck by how wonderful this felt, taking time in the middle of the week to do something she loved, with the person she loved most in the world.

She couldn't help herself and reached out, touching Neva's cheek.

"You have a little something there…"

Neva laughed. "You know you don't have to cosplay a scene from a Hallmark movie just to kiss me…"

"No?"

"No. Any time you want works for me." So, she did lean in and kiss her, softly at first, then a bit more passionately, until two enthusiastic children interrupted them.

"Cookies!" Fiona sang.

"Can we help? Please?" Elsa asked.

"Yes, definitely," Angie declared. "We can use all the help we can get."

She was going to get her life back. It was going to happen.

·♥·♥·♥·♥·♥·

Later that night she stood in the bedroom, daring a quick glance at the gift she had bought for Neva. She held the necklace in her hands, examining it from all sides.

If you have any magic power, please, give me back my life.
Only you can do that, Nadine's words echoed on her mind.

But how? She hastily put the gift back in its hiding place when she heard Neva coming out of the bathroom and got under the covers.

"That was nice earlier, baking with the girls," Neva said with a smile as she joined Angie in bed.

"Yes, it was," Angie confirmed, the memory putting a smile on her face despite herself. They had put the cookies aside for dinner, and Fiona and Elsa had been happy to help decorating afterwards. That's when it *did* become a mess, but somehow no one minded.

Right track. She was so sure.

She was also relieved that neither Christina nor her parents seemed to have contacted Neva about her calls. She could operate in secret a little while longer...While getting the Christmas underway that they would all enjoy.

One way or another.

Chapter Ten

NEVA

N eva figured that perhaps she had relied too much on the idea that after all the big changes they had made, there couldn't be others happening soon. They had eased into their lives and routines, made some compromises, and sacrifices even, all for the greater good.

Now, days before Christmas, Angie wanted to mix it all up, and she wasn't sure how she felt about it. Routines were safe for both of them in a world where much wasn't.

Parenting came with surprises and new challenges at every corner. It was good to be able to hold on to something, wasn't it?

She appreciated Angie taking time off, but at the same time she was worried that she might fill that time with all kinds of activities the way it was before and burn herself out again. It was for a good reason that they maintained the clean, quiet house, that Christina could attend Caron Academy. They had worked hard for it, and she didn't want to go back to a place of doubt.

Strange that an evening of baking and decorating cookies would have her worried, but in fact, she hadn't stopped since that strange dinner. Dr. McEwen's assessment was a huge relief. Other than that, she was running out of ideas, though she had to admit, she was looking forward to Christmas dinner with her parents.

Something she wasn't looking forward to, at all, was confronting Angie about her conversation with Caron's principal, but that could wait.

As she was driving home after dropping off Fiona and Elsa at school, her sister called.

"I need a big favor."

"What's the matter?" She still needed to get in a few hours of work today, but Neva figured she would be fine unless Angie had planned another baking spree.

"You know that we've been fostering a litter of kittens..." Amanda sounded apologetic.

Neva had to admit she had almost forgotten about it. She distantly remembered that she had promised to take Fiona and Elsa to see them sometime, but she still had to run it by Angie. "From your neighbor who moved away, right? The cat's name was...Coconut. You said you had found homes for all of them, didn't you?"

"Yes, Coco's. They kept one of them, but we handled the adoptions for the rest. The last one kind of fell through...And you know we won't be home for Christmas. I've asked around, but I couldn't find anyone."

"Oh, Amanda, this is tricky. You know Angie is allergic."

This conversation felt like a strange déjà vu. Why had Angie thought they already had a cat? It had to be a coincidence. Nothing else made sense.

"I know, and I'm really sorry. But you have the space, so maybe they don't have to run into each other?" Amanda asked, her tone hopeful.

"I have to ask her, okay? I'll call you back."

Once upon a time, they had fantasized about a house full of children and pets. Reality had caught up to them quickly.

Neva pulled into their driveway and went inside the house, lost in thought. Amanda was right, they might be able to avoid contact between Angie and the kitten. She hesitated doing this at a moment when Angie wasn't quite herself, and besides, if there was a kitten in the house for Christmas, it was never going to leave. The girls wouldn't have it—or they would be forever disappointed in them.

What to do?

She called Angie to share her dilemma.

"A kitten?" Angie sounded almost...enthusiastic about it? Neva shook her head, perplexed. "You know it's not the best idea, with your allergies. And we know the girls love you, but once they see the cute face, I'm afraid they won't care."

"That's possible." Angie laughed. "But Amanda has no one to take care of it."

"Not really. I feel bad. I'd also feel bad if I'm responsible for you sniffling and sneezing the entire holiday."

"Look, I don't even know for sure if it would be that bad. How about we all go for a visit tonight and give it a try?"

"Are you sure?" The moment the twins laid eyes on the kitten, they'd be gone, and Neva and Angie would have no choice.

"Yes. I'd like to try. Unless...do we know how Brad is with cats?"

"Curious. Not hostile as far as I know. I'll invite us over, then?"

"Yes, please do. We haven't seen them in a while either. Besides, I have tomorrow off. Let's do it."

Neva still couldn't believe it when she shared the news with her overjoyed sister.

"Of course, let's have dinner! I owe you."

Well, it was Christmas. Miracles and other strange, wondrous occurrences happened, didn't they?

Chapter Eleven

ANGIE

She could sense that Neva was still confused about the changes she had introduced, about her own apparent sudden change of mind. She had to admit, remembering coming home to a chaotic house and a new pet had made her cranky that other time...Given the challenge thrust upon her, it was important to keep the big picture in mind.

By the time they got closer to Amanda's place, she was almost as excited as the twins in the backseat. It was almost Christmas. Which put more pressure on her to find a solution, but how could she not when it was her favorite holiday?

She had reacted badly that other time she had encountered the kitten. She wouldn't make the same mistake again. Maybe it was as simple as that?

They drove past decorated houses and trees, snow people in creative attire, past suburban neighborhoods to the more rural area where Amanda and her husband lived. Closer to their property, the road tightened, the snow piled high on either side.

The couple had made room for their guests to park in front, and the four of them headed for the entrance where Amanda opened the door to them.

"Hey! I haven't seen you in too long!" she exclaimed. "You've grown so much since the last time."

She said that to the twins every time, Angie reflected, but this time it might actually be true. Neva and Amanda talked on the phone regularly, but there hadn't been much time for a visit in months.

I understand it now. I'm sorry I didn't make more time for family, and I will.

The moment she walked through the door, Angie realized that nothing seemed to have changed in Amanda's reality. Even though they were only three people in the house (now often two, since Kristen was in college), it was never quiet, laughter, music, pets.

She remembered a time when it felt too much for her, but now, her own home with the constant quiet seemed lifeless in comparison.

Had she really killed the mood that often? It would change, she vowed. For starters, she wouldn't stand in the way of—

"Oh, and who's that?"

She crouched down to carefully reach out to the fluffy bundle walking towards her. The kitten sniffed her fingers curiously. Angie waited a few more heartbeats before she picked it up. "She's so light," she said, in awe.

Fluffy. She looked just as Angie remembered. Not that she would mention it to Neva.

"I'm so glad you can take care of her for a few days," Amanda said. "But are you sure you'll be okay with your allergies?"

"It was a long time ago. Maybe I don't even have them anymore," Angie dismissed her concerns, aware of Neva's worried gaze.

"Mommy, can we hold her?"

The kitten seemed to be very comfortable in her arms, but Angie reminded herself she should be careful. Just in case.

"Sure, but be gentle, okay?"

She was proud to see that both Fiona and Elsa handled the small animal with the required tenderness. Of course, having two puppies in the house from a young age helped.

No, one puppy. Brad. She could feel the first stirrings of a headache and decided to ignore it. Enjoying dinner with family was the first step to coming home. Bringing Fluffy with them, another.

She couldn't wait to see Nadine again and tell her that this time, she had handled "Kittengate" so much better.

·♥·♥·♥·♥·♥·

Angie's enthusiasm was slightly diminished once they were home and getting ready for bed. Her headache hadn't improved, and her allergy had come knocking.

"You know that they're counting on us to keep the kitten, right? The puppy dog eyes will be worse than Brad's."

"I know, and I'm—" *Sneeze.* "Okay with that." *Sneeze.* "I swear."

"Oh, Angie."

Neva brushed a cool hand over her forehead, a welcome soothing gesture that distracted her from the discomfort of her prickling skin and runny nose.

Yes, it was her fault. Yes, she should have known better than becoming closely acquainted with the kitten and trying to push back the first signs with plenty of the rich red wine Amanda had offered for dinner. Too little too late now.

She was trying, wasn't she? Again, things hadn't quite worked out like she had hoped, but her efforts had to be rewarded at some point.

"I'm really sorry," she sniffed. "But if they want to keep her, it's okay. I'll ask Dr. McEwen for a new prescription." She'd had one for an antihistamine before, Angie remembered, though that had nothing to do with cats.

"That took a while to work the last time. I don't want you to be miserable 24/7," Neva declared. "And I was kidding. I'm sorry too. They will understand."

"I don't want to disappoint them." At least Neva's magic touch seemed to have gotten the sneezing attacks under control, but Angie still sounded pathetic to her own ears.

"They'll be fine, and they want you to be okay too. How about we wait until Amanda is back, and we decide then?"

"Okay."

Neva lay down next to her, and after she'd turned off the lights, they gravitated towards each other like always. Angie was still puzzled, still wondering how all of this was even possible.

·♥·♥·♥·♥·♥·

Unfortunately, she found out the next morning that her allergy was still very real. The girls had noticed it too, exchanging glances, expressing their enthusiasm about the house guest in a quieter way.

What was the right thing to do? How could she find a way to make everyone happy and still stay healthy?

Questions pressing against her mind, she had snuck out of bed early and made waffles, then a generous breakfast spread. Maybe part of her wanted to prepare everyone that Kitten might have to go, maybe she just needed to indulge herself. It worked both ways.

"Mom," Fiona said, looking far too serious for her age. "Is Kitty making you sick?"

"Really, it's not that bad," Angie hurried to respond.

"Angie."

"Yes."

She half-sighed, interrupted by another sneeze. "We'll keep her at least until Amanda is back. She can go in your room."

Elsa all but leapt off her chair to hug her. "Thank you. Maybe you'll be fine in a few days."

Angie doubted it, but it looked like she'd successfully stalled the conversation for a bit longer. Good. She had bigger issues to deal with.

Like, maybe they should get another dog?

The thought almost made her smile though she was aware that she had only little time left to solve the riddle, and if she couldn't, then what?

Angie looked around the table, wondering what would happen if she failed, and stayed in this reality forever. She saw Neva's worried gaze and could sense that the girls were aware of the tension too, even with the happy news. And Christina at Caron.

No, simply keeping Fluffy wouldn't solve anything.

She needed a big gesture, something, well, life-changing.

If only she knew what that gesture was...

Chapter Twelve

NEVA

She wasn't sure what Angie was thinking, making this kind of promises so close to Christmas, but Neva would put her foot down once Amanda could take the kitten again. The twins would be sad, for sure, and she felt a bit irritated with Angie for making them hope they could keep it.

There was just no way she could watch Angie suffer the way she had known she would.

The problem was, Neva was running out of options. She imagined things would improve once they went back to normal after the holidays, but she didn't want to rush her family through them either.

Angie loved Christmas.

They all did.

There had to be a way to make it merry for everyone, without stress or pressure.

For the twins, it was the last day of school, and Christina would be home tonight. They had busy days ahead, and yet

Neva felt herself drawn to a cabinet in the basement she hadn't opened in years. Because they had decided on a different path together, and there was no more room or time.

The paint in those tubes was dried out, but she found a sketchbook and some pencils. The sketchbook was half-filled. Neva both frowned and smiled at sketches she didn't remember creating, then felt the warmth of tears in her eyes, from an emotion hard to define. A mix of wistfulness, gratitude...and love.

Her family, Brad included, often made an appearance. Angie had always been her muse. Neva had fallen for her the first time they met in the small-town diner where Neva had spent the day people-watching and looking for inspiration, and Angie squeezed in time for a small coffee break.

Neva flipped to an empty page and sat down in an armchair, pencil in hand. She didn't have time for this trip down memory lane, but she couldn't resist it either.

She continued until her ringing phone startled her, and then she hastily put away the sketchbook. There was no time for this.

"Hello?"

"Hi." Angie sounded as guilty as Neva felt. "I'm sorry, but I'll be late today. I have to catch up on work and then a few errands after that."

"Oh. Are you sure you're not avoiding the kitten? The last word has not yet been spoken on the issue, I promise."

"Thank you, but no. I'll be okay. Could you pick up Christina from the bus station?"

"You won't be joining us?" This was strange after the way Angie had been acting about Christina attending Caron.

"I still might, but I can't promise anything. We could all go out for dinner?"

"I guess that works. See you later. Love you."

"Love you too," Angie said before she ended the call.

Neva still had so many questions, but she had to figure out the logistics for the rest of the day. A look at her watch told her it was time to pick up Fiona and Elsa. First things first. Christmas would come either way, whether they were ready or not.

When she arrived at the school, the twins were hyped up on holiday cheer and anticipation for Christmas activities and the big day arriving soon.

To Neva's relief, they didn't ask about the kitten. She wasn't sure whether they were just stalling but she would take it.

"Hey, how about we go get Christina, and then we can have lunch at the Christmas market?"

Angie must be rubbing off on her. They were always so careful to have the kids eat right and not overdo it on sweets...but this was only once a year, wasn't it?

Besides, Neva felt like a sweet indulgence herself.

"Can we have churros with caramel?" Elsa asked hopefully.

So be it.

"Sure. Let's go, and later we will go on a long walk with Brad to make sure we are still hungry for dinner."

The twins laughed at her words. Neva was wondering what errands Angie had been talking about, but she didn't have time to dwell on it either. They stopped at home to leave the girls' schoolbags before she drove them all to the bus station. A huge tree stood in the lobby, sparkling with many lights and ornaments.

Despite all the current challenges, she felt excited seeing the wonder in the girls' eyes, happy they'd have Christina home for a bit. Everything would work itself out, wouldn't it?

She looked past the tree at the board that announced the bus's arrival.

"Come on," she said, taking both girls by the hand. "Let's go get your sister."

· ♥ · ♥ · ♥ · ♥ · ♥ ·

Christina all but flew at them, hugging first her sisters, then Neva.

"I'm so glad to be here!"

Neva could sympathize. She hugged her oldest daughter tightly.

"And we're happy to have you here. Are you up for having lunch at the market?"

"Always. Isn't Mom here?" The smile vanished from Christina's face. "Is she okay? She's been acting weird."

Tell me about it, Neva thought, feeling instantly guilty.

"She's fine, just working overtime. We'll all go out for dinner later."

Christina nodded. Her expression was much too restrained, too adult, and Neva had a hard time gauging if she was satisfied with the answer. Regardless, she had to feed all of them now.

The bus station was almost close enough to the Christmas market to have delicious smells wafting over to them, or perhaps that was her imagination. She could use some indulgence. Everything else, they'd address later.

They left the car at the station and walked on foot, music and anticipated smells greeting them soon. First stop was the churros stand. Neva knew the twins would be hyped up on sugar, but they had a few days left before Christmas, and the market with all its excitement came around only once a year so...

She would have to be okay with it, and strangely, Neva realized, she was. Many things were different this year. She and Angie had built a life on caution, on making sure there was enough to give their children the best possible life. One little slip wasn't going to break the bank or their daughters' health.

They walked past the generously decorated merry-go-round and the wooden German-inspired Christmas pyramid to the other side where more food stands were located alongside arts and crafts.

Neva noticed that Christina had gone silent, taking in the familiar sights. They tried to make it at least once a season, though with her coming home later from Caron, it hadn't worked out the previous year. This was something else that made her feel guilty now, even though Christina had always stressed how happy she was at the prestigious boarding school.

"Everything okay, sweetie?" she asked. She had to raise her voice slightly above *Jingle Bells* coming from the speakers.

"Yeah, sure, just a little tired," Christina said with a shrug. "What are we having?"

"What do you feel like?"

"For real?"

"Yes, for real."

Neva glanced from her to the twins who had, despite their best efforts and a pile of napkins, caramel on their fingers and cheeks reddened from excitement and the cold. They looked happy.

She was too, with Angie and their family, though she couldn't help thinking she was missing something. Her little trip down memory lane, picking up that pencil again, had shaken her. She missed painting.

"So, what will it be?"

"I think I want the cheese fondue. They would never serve that at Caron."

"Well, once a year is perfectly fine."

She produced some wet wipes so Fiona and Elsa could get a little less sticky, and they moved on to the cheese fondue. Neva had some too, and she made sure that sweet wasn't all the twins ate.

They were about ready to head back to the car when she stopped cold.

In another corner was a jewelry stand, the vendor someone familiar: Nadine, their neighbor whom Angie had brought to dinner the other day. On whose door she had pounded for some never-explained reason. The woman leaning close to her, whispering, was...Angie?

What did that mean?

Neva felt her face flush when her mind went to all kinds of worst-case scenarios as to why Angie was so close with the jeweler. She wasn't in her right mind. Neva knew that Angie was loyal to the core, that she loved her.

More likely, she was looking for a gift. That made sense. That's why she was working late, because she used her lunch break for an errand. Right?

In that case, Neva shouldn't let it on that she'd seen her.

Everything was all right.

They'd still go out to eat tonight, have her parents come over for Christmas Eve dinner and see Angie's for lunch before they went on their cruise.

Everything according to plan.

"Okay, let's head home, girls. I have a bit of work to do before we meet Mom for dinner."

Fiona laughed. "That's okay, we are not hungry!"

"I bet you aren't. Come on. Let's go."

She wasn't sure how to interpret Christina's expression.

Chapter Thirteen

ANGIE

"Isn't there anything you can do? I made a mess in the kitchen, and we got another cute pet. She's making me sneeze a lot, but I can live with that. I tried to have a big family dinner, but my parents already booked their vacation. That wasn't up to me, was it? Please, what else can I do?!"

Distantly, Angie was aware that she had to sound like a madwoman, but catching Nadine at the Christmas market seemed like the only avenue left since she still hadn't come up with a better idea. This place was associated with the holiday more than anything. It was worth a try, wasn't it? She was running out of options and time.

Nadine regarded her with sympathy after carefully arranging her display of bracelets, earrings and necklaces.

"You are trying so hard you're missing the most obvious thing."

"And what would that be? If you know it, why aren't you telling me? That's cruel."

Nadine shook her head. "No, it just *is*. That's different from cruel. You're in this situation because you made a wish. You wanted things to be different. Now they are, and if you're not happy, you should ask yourself why."

"I know why!" Angie leaned closer, because she didn't want the woman perusing the merchandise to overhear her, and besides, if she lowered her voice, she might sound a little less absurd. "Everything seems so...wiped clean. We used to have so much fun together, to be close, and happy, and now everyone's walking on eggshells all the time. Christina doesn't talk to me anymore. I used to be able to tell if everyone was happy, and now I can't, and...it hurts."

"You have a few more days to figure it out," Nadine said. "I wish you the best of luck. Merry Christmas, Angie. Please excuse me."

When she went to address the potential customer, Angie left, tears blurring her vision.

She had to keep it together, go back to work and then home, all cheery for the family dinner.

Or maybe she needed to tell Neva the truth.

·♥·♥·♥·♥·♥·

The thought was so unsettling she dismissed it right away, but it lingered during the day, as she tried to concentrate on work, and later when she drove home.

Angie was excited to see Christina and worried at the same time. She and Neva had always wanted to make it clear that the girls could tell them everything. They meant it. Sure, now Christina had friends she confided in, but something was still off.

Well, surprise. Her entire life was "off" at this moment, and she didn't have the slightest clue how to fix it. Nadine's question had stirred something up though. Why wasn't she happy?

What grand gesture could she make to restore the life she knew?

With some trepidation, she let herself into the house. It was quiet, though when she walked further inside, she could see light from Neva's office and hear the twins laugh in their room. Brad was sleeping in his dog bed, and Fluffy was nowhere to be seen.

Angie couldn't ignore her presence though, the instant sneeze reminding her.

She went straight to Neva's office, and Neva got up to greet her with a kiss.

"Hi. You're still at work?"

"Just finishing something up. How was your day?"

Neva was smiling, so how could Angie hear an edge in her voice?

"Good. Long. I'll just change, and we can go eat? I'm starving."

"Sure, but it's okay if you take your time. I need a few more minutes, and we had lunch at the Christmas market."

"Oh." Angie wasn't sure what else to say. She was lucky they hadn't caught her badgering Nadine.

"We talked about this on the phone, remember?" Now there was definitely an edge.

"Yes, I know, but...I hope they didn't have too much sugar."

Where did that come from? Angie froze, realizing she was acting more like this reality's version of herself than the one she wanted to get back to. Neva had noticed it too.

"I thought you said a bit of indulgence around the holidays was fine. It was just to welcome Christina."

"I'm sorry I couldn't be there. I'll get ready."

"Yeah."

Angie left the room, closed the door behind her, and walked a few steps only to jump when she nearly ran into Christina. How much of her and Neva's argument had she overheard? Angie's face heated at the possibilities. Sure, she and Neva disagreed sometimes, but they had a strict rule of not arguing in front of the girls.

Nevertheless, she was happy and relieved to see Christina. Angie folded her daughter into a tight embrace.

"You're home! I missed you so much."

Christina held on. Sometimes, gestures were easier than words. Angie could relate.

"Is everything okay?" she asked quietly.

"You tell me."

To her surprise, Christina sounded almost angry when she stepped back.

"What's going on?"

"You call me at school, in the middle of class, when you knew I was coming home for Christmas. And you asked me if I liked being at Caron, with the principal sitting right across from me. It was embarrassing! Why would you do that when you couldn't wait for me to go there?"

For the second time today, Angie was close to tears. This wasn't about her though, and it was too important for her to worry about her own feelings.

"We thought that was what you wanted too! We would have never sent you if you weren't okay with it, Christina. Did something happen?"

"Whatever." Christina turned around, then thought twice about it. "No, nothing happened, except that weird call. I'm sorry, Mom, but please don't do that again?"

"I promise," Angie said quickly.

That moment, the kitten zipped by at a remarkable speed, perhaps startled by something.

"Wait, who's the fluffy comet?" Christina asked, in awe. "A kitten? I thought you were allergic?"

"Aunt Amanda needed someone to take care of her for a little while." Angie kept the timeline vague on purpose. The last thing she needed was to disappoint anyone else.

"Okay." Christina stepped closer and back into her embrace. "I'm sorry. I missed you too."

"It's okay. We'll have a few days together. And we'll start with a nice dinner."

"Good luck." Christina laughed. "I think everyone's still a bit full from lunch."

"That was hours ago! How much did you all eat?"

Christina's laughter was worth it, making her forget that she'd skipped lunch trying to fix this mess. Angie was still teetering on the edge, but she was determined to keep calm this evening. Stick to the plan. Figure out what to do.

"I guess I'll hear about it. I'll get ready, and worst-case scenario, you can all accompany me and watch me eat." She hesitated. "Are you really okay?"

"I swear. Now, shouldn't you get going?"

Angie took the hint.

Something still told her that she should share her predicament with someone else, that Nadine shouldn't be the only one. It seemed like the jeweler wasn't affected by the outcome either way.

If Angie couldn't figure it out, maybe the person she loved most in the world could?

·❦·❦·❦·❦·❦·

By the time they got to dinner, everyone else was in the mood for food again. Over pizza, they shared plans for the coming days, and Christina opened up a bit more, talking about her friends and favorite subjects in school.

Angie listened closely, somewhat reassured to know that she was doing well, academically and socially. Nothing to worry about, right? Until she reminded herself that this wasn't reality, but a disorienting copy of it.

Neva had to feel it too.

Later that night, when they had retreated to their bedroom, Angie found new resolve and hope. Perhaps this was what had been in front of her all along. She had to come clean, about everything.

"Neva," she said.

"Hm?" her wife answered with a sleepy sound.

"I'm sorry, but I have to talk to you. It's urgent."

Neva, now wide awake, sat up in bed and stared at her. She looked worried, no, more scared, illuminated by the fairy lights they had decorated their bedroom with.

"Something happened the other day…" She hesitated for a heartbeat. And then some more. "With Nadine. I'm sorry, Neva but I need to talk about this."

"What happened? What did she do?"

Angie took a deep breath. "It's more about something I did," she said, feeling her eyes well up. "And I'm so, so sorry. It's important that you know—"

Neva, who had been listening quietly until now, held up a hand, shocked disbelief in her expression. "No. Maybe it isn't. Angie, why, what were you thinking? I don't want to hear this, not now, not ever."

"What do you mean?"

"I'm going to need a moment," Neva declared as she got up. "And I don't want to hear the details."

"Wait, what?" The blood shot to her face when she realized what Neva meant. "Oh my God. That's not it! I would never! I...I can't believe you're thinking that."

Neva's face flushed. "You didn't...All right. You didn't. I'm so sorry!" Sitting back down, she sounded relieved and embarrassed at the same time, as she wiped a hand over her face. "I can't believe it either. You've been so stressed lately, and I was afraid... but that's no excuse either. Please, can we start over? Forgive me?"

Obviously, they would have to, but why would Neva even go there? That was perhaps a question for another day, though it seemed to fit right into this confusing alternate universe. What Angie actually had to tell her should be much easier in comparison. But it wasn't, and she chose to stall.

"Yes, I forgive you, but I reserve the right to bring that up in a fight ten or twenty years down the line, okay?"

Neva laughed softly. "I'm an idiot, and you have every right to bring it up as often as you'd like. When I saw you at the market..."

"You saw me? Why didn't you just come over...Okay, let's put a pin in that for now. This does have to do with Nadine though." She couldn't put it off any longer. "Remember the day I brought her to dinner? When we parked out front, I saw that the string of lights on the tree was broken again, and..." In hindsight, it seemed silly that this one little thing had led her to want to alter the course of her life.

In the future, Angie would be *extremely* careful what she wished for.

"It made me think of all the things we still had to do before Christmas, and I won't lie, I got a little mad, and frustrated, and I made a wish."

"You made a wish. Okay."

The blank look on Neva's face told Angie that she had to give her a few more details, and quick.

"Anyway, everything seemed so messy at the time. You had just brought Fluffy home, and we still had to make more cookies and get wrapping paper…" It came to her that Neva had apparently no memory of these events, as in this reality, they didn't bake cookies and had their gifts wrapped at the store. To Angie's relief, Neva played along.

"So, what did you wish for?" she asked.

"The perfect Christmas." Angie took a deep breath. "I was childish, but I thought it would be nice to have one holiday where everything was already in place, no messes, no working around the clock to make it happen…I'm so sorry. I was ungrateful. Then we walked in, and everything had changed. And now I don't know how to get it back."

"Get what back, Angie? You're not making sense." The emotion coming off her voice was a mix of concern and fear, but not for herself. Neva reached out to touch Angie's forehead, making her shrink back.

"I know! But this is what happened. I just wanted a break. I blinked and everything changed. Our daughter is in boarding school, no one laughs at dinner, you don't paint anymore, and…you thought I was having an affair!"

Neva was silent for long moments.

"I don't know what to say," she finally spoke. "Except for me jumping to conclusions. I shouldn't have. I don't know why I said it, and I am truly sorry. The rest…those are all things we agreed on, to make life easier for us, but mostly for the kids, so they can succeed. And it might be a small detail, but given everything that has happened, I think I should remind you that we didn't yet have the kitten when Nadine came to dinner. Wait, why did you call her Fluffy?"

So she had noticed.

"That's what I'm trying to tell you! I named her. This was in the other reality. Our life. Our real life, where we are happy, and Christina isn't in boarding school, and we have three pets..." Angie forced herself to take a breath. "I was hoping you could help me, that we could brainstorm together? If we don't figure it out by midnight on Christmas Eve, it will stay like this forever. That's what Nadine told me. I've been trying to get her to help me ever since."

"Angie!" Neva took her hands, holding on so tightly it was almost painful, desperate to make her point. "I don't know what's gotten into you, but *this* is our life. The only one we have. I am so sorry you're not happy."

She was a heartbeat away from tears. Angie was, too. She had to make sure Neva understood. So much depended on it. Maybe...everything.

"That's not what I said. I said..."

"You made a wish and catapulted all of us into an alternate reality." There was resignation to her tone now.

"It sounds weird when you put it like that, but yes. Nadine is...what she called, a wish granter. And when I said it out loud, she made it happen, and she claims she can't undo it."

"What does she say?"

"That I have to find the solution. I'm running out of ideas."

Angie had harbored the hope that Neva might be at least curious.

"It's been a long day. Perhaps we should get some sleep."

"I've been trying to get us back, take more time off, bake cookies, have our parents over, but whatever I do, it's not the right thing. I needed to talk to you."

Neva reached out, brushing her fingers over Angie's cheek, before she kissed her softly.

"You can always talk to me, but now, I think you need some rest. Please, trust me on this. Everything will look different in the morning."

Her tone lacked conviction, but it was clear to Angie that the conversation was over for tonight. She had to try again, find a better angle. Tomorrow.

When Neva opened her arms, she went eagerly.

They hadn't solved anything, but it was a first step.

And they still had twenty-four hours.

Chapter Fourteen

NEVA

S he had hoped that Christina's arrival would help calm things down. Apparently, that was not the case, and with them expecting her own parents tonight, Neva didn't know what to do.

Of course, she believed Angie when she said she wasn't cheating on her, but there was something else going on with Nadine. She still flushed with embarrassment at the memory of blurting out those words, showing her how much she, too, had been on edge.

The whole story about the wish granting?

Neva almost wanted to call Dr. McEwen again, if only to hear that she had nothing to worry about. At this point, she found it hard to believe, given that Angie had been talking about alternate realities and wanting a messy house.

Okay, that wasn't exactly what she had said, but it sounded disturbing enough.

What should she do? Pretend this strange conversation had never happened? It seemed to matter a lot to Angie.

She had also mentioned Neva's painting, and yes, Neva missed it too. Maybe they were overdue to talk more in depth about things they had been taken for granted in recent years.

Without a doubt, the timing was exceptionally bad. Neva didn't want Angie to think she was brushing her off, but she also didn't know what to add to the words they'd said. Having a Christmas Eve dinner had been Angie's wish, so for the next couple of days, she wanted to be the wish granter and provide holiday cheer for their family. That, Neva was confident, would make Angie happy. And then they could talk.

She shook her head at the idea that Angie would prefer chaos. That was not how they had designed their lives. They had wanted safety, some predictability. Caron Academy produced predictable results. The way they were raising their children did, didn't it?

And she would have to talk to Amanda about the kitten—Fluffy?—because Neva ignoring last night's conversation at breakfast couldn't be all the reason for the redness around Angie's eyes. At least she hoped it wasn't the case.

"So, who's going to come with me for last-minute shopping?"

Everyone confirmed with varying degrees. The twins were always happy to go to decorated stores and supermarkets, no matter how loud or crowded. Christina acted more casual, but to Neva's relief she could see the excitement in her eyes.

She was approaching adulthood far too fast. At least they would have her home for a little while. Angie looked tired, but she smiled. Neva read it as an agreement that they wouldn't raise any complicated subjects for the moment.

Perfect. The real holidays could begin—well, after they had all the ingredients to impress her parents tonight.

It had been years since they'd cooked a big spread together, and Neva was in equal parts excited and terrified, especially when she saw the line at the first supermarket. Maybe catering wouldn't have been the worst idea?

·♥·♥·♥·♥·♥·

She had to admit Angie was holding up better than she'd thought, navigating them through the madness part of the holiday, sales and indulgences and everything they needed for their dinner while making sure the kids were involved.

Neva found herself wondering if it could always be like this, if Christina wasn't at Caron.

But that would be selfish of them, wouldn't it? Just like it would be selfish to take up painting again, out of the blue, a hobby, when they needed both incomes to support the lives they had.

Finally, they were back home where they started preparing dinner while the girls were setting the table.

"This is new," Christina remarked, standing in the doorway. "I mean it's nice that Grandma and Grandpa are coming over, but we don't usually do that."

"I thought it would be nice to shake things up a bit," Angie answered, adorable in an apron that Neva had never seen before, with a couple of penguins under a glittering star on it. "Mom and Dad already booked a cruise, but we'll see them for a quick lunch tomorrow."

"Okay. The table is set. Anything else you want me to do?"

"It's fine. Unless you want to peel a few more potatoes."

Christina's face said it all.

"You can keep an eye on Fluffy and make sure she stays out of the kitchen," Neva said. At the moment, the kitten was with the twins whom she seemed to like best of the family. Angie came second, and Fluffy tended to seek her out. They'd find a solution after Christmas.

For now, it was best to go with the flow.

"I can do that," Christina agreed and left.

Momentarily alone, the silence was stretching between them even in the busy atmosphere. Neva stepped closer to Angie and kissed her softly.

"What was that for?" Angie asked, surprised.

"Just because. Merry Christmas."

A smile lit up Angie's face. "Merry Christmas, my love."

It would be all right. Everything else was unthinkable.

···♥·♥·♥·♥·♥··

Her parents arrived a little after 4 p.m., laden with gifts they added to the small mountain already under their tree.

"This is so nice," her mom said, hugging her tightly. "Spending Christmas with all of my favorite girls."

She looked so happy Neva felt a pang of guilt for not doing this earlier. She had assumed everyone, including her parents and Angie, would enjoy some quiet over the holidays, not having to spend substantial parts of them in the kitchen. Today had been fun, though.

Perhaps she and Angie were both a little confused this year. They had worked hard as always. It might be time to reconsider some things, though none if it explained the story of their neighbor Nadine doing weird magic for Christmas.

"Laura, hi. Harry. We're glad you're here," Angie greeted them. "Have a seat. Would you like something to drink?"

After getting the affirmative, they got everyone settled in the living room, and Angie went to the kitchen to make hot chocolate for the girls, and a spiced eggnog for the adults.

Neva followed her, leaning against the island, for a moment amazed how confidently Angie had breezed through all of today's challenges, after nearly breaking down last night. This was their life. The right one. The real one. Wasn't it?

She studied her for a moment, once again torn between the certainty that nothing could tear them apart, and the worry of not knowing what was going on.

Because Nadine was their neighbor and a talented jeweler, nothing more.

"Aren't you going to help?" Angie asked, amusement in her voice.

"Yes. Of course. What do you need?"

Angie turned to her with a tray of mugs filled with deliciously smelling hot beverages.

"Too late. But you can bring the whipped cream and the sprinkles."

"Angie, I just want to say I'm sorry." She had no idea why it was coming out now, this way, when she'd been determined to keep things merry.

"That's okay." Angie looked pensive. "There might be some things I forgot to tell you last night, but we'll talk about it later, okay? I know it all sounds bizarre, but I swear this is what Nadine told me. There is still a way to fix this."

Disappointed, Neva plastered a smile on her face. So, she wasn't going to let this go anytime soon. And what would happen when the clock struck twelve and they'd still be in the same reality they'd always been in? What would Angie do?

·♥·♥·♥·♥·♥·

She had come to check on dinner when she realized the door to their guestroom was open, voices coming from inside. Neva had tried to focus on what was most important, their family together, but Angie's refusal to give up on her strange story lingered on her mind.

How far would she go with it?

She opened the door a bit, not meaning to eavesdrop, but when she saw Christina was crying, Neva went inside right away.

"What happened?"

"I knew it. I knew something was up." Angie's eyes were red-rimmed once more, and not just because Christina was clutching Fluffy.

Brad sat at her feet. Neva thought he looked like he was worried too.

Didn't Angie say something about another dog? And she was convinced they had gotten Fluffy on the day she brought Nadine to dinner. Nothing made sense.

"I didn't want to say anything because...You work so hard all the time, just so I can go there. And for the most part it's fine, but I don't like what they've been saying about you. And no one punishes them for it."

Oh no.

When they had first met with the principal, the school seemed open-minded and welcoming. She and Angie had found no red flags whenever they introduced themselves as Angie's parents.

"They are legacy students, so no one will touch them. But I won't be silent," Christina insisted. "This is my family."

"Of course, honey." Neva finally moved and hugged her. "I promise you, we'll talk to the principal right after the holidays."

"I don't think that will do much," Angie spoke up. "We still can, but the principal told her to stay quiet. I don't like this at all. I want Christina to come home."

This was all going far too fast for Neva.

"I understand you're upset, but we have to find a moment to talk this through," she said. "To make a plan."

"I'm sorry," Christina sniffed. "I didn't mean to ruin Christmas."

"You didn't," Neva assured her. "We'll figure this out."

"What's to figure out?" There was an edge to Angie's voice. "She's not going back. I knew this was a bad idea to begin with."

"Really?" Neva's good intentions went out the window. "It was your idea!"

"That's not true."

"But it is. Look, I'm not blaming you. I'm just saying—" She halted when Christina jumped to her feet and left the room, but not before setting Fluffy gently on her chair. The kitten meowed softly, and Angie sneezed. She still looked incredulous, as if she didn't remember.

Maybe she didn't.

"Angie, please, let's take a breath, okay? We've had a few stressful weeks. Let's take it one day at a time, please?"

"You still don't believe me."

"I believe you that you think all of it is true, Nadine, the wish, but the truth is we have some decisions to make."

"Christina being unhappy isn't my imagination. It never was. And you miss painting. I know you do."

"That has nothing to do with me."

"I'm trying to help." Angie sounded desperate. "If we don't get this right, and soon, we won't have any more chances."

"To do what? Do you really hate our life so much?"

"You don't understand."

"No. Maybe I don't." Nadine, Caron, painting, the choices and the sacrifices they'd made, it was all too much to deal with at the moment, while they were supposed to be serving the main course. "Scratch that, I definitely don't understand."

"Okay." Angie wiped her hand over her eyes and turned towards the door.

"Where are you going?"

"To get some fresh air. I need to clear my head."

"Now?"

She didn't get an answer. Neva couldn't help the searing feeling that she'd missed an important moment—even if she still didn't believe in the wish granter. But she wished things were different, and that Angie would turn around and come home.

The sound of the front door opening and closing told her otherwise.

Chapter Fifteen

ANGIE

It wasn't until she sat in the car that Angie realized what she was doing. Sort of. She had no idea where she was going, but she knew she had to think, and ironically, it wasn't possible in her home, with the people she loved.

She would have to come home eventually, and clean up the mess she'd made, and it wouldn't be easy.

Neva didn't believe her.

Christina was the target of teen cruelty and adult ignorance, and above all, she wanted to help her.

She wanted to turn back time. It seemed so silly now to cry about a few broken lights, about how many batches of cookies were the right amount, and the generally busy days leading up to Christmas.

Neva, in this reality, couldn't know, but once upon a time they had already gotten it right. And Angie would give it one last try. If she couldn't make it, she would spend the rest of her life trying to convince her family how much she loved them, that they didn't need to fit their holidays into a mold to be happy.

She shook her head to herself.

It sounded bizarre. She wouldn't have believed herself.

It didn't make sense. Nothing made sense, her being out here while families celebrated Christmas Eve, and she could be doing the same, see the excitement in her children's eyes as they wondered if their wishes would come true.

Angie laughed bitterly. *Be careful what you wish for*...So true. It didn't help that every house along the way was decorated, the neighborhood looking cozy with the softly falling snow.

She should be home, but she couldn't be right now.

Something was drawing her to the mall, even though she knew that most of the businesses would be closed. The diner might still be open, though she was far from hungry for food.

Walking back through these doors, Angie wasn't sure what her plan was, except that this was where it all had started. Her constant stressing about this and that, getting Neva's Christmas gift in time. The accident she'd seen on the way. She couldn't help shuddering. Angie hoped the family impacted by it was okay and was having a merry time right now.

She pulled her coat tighter around her and walked past dark stores and other businesses.

Nadine's, like the others, had a "Closed" sign in the front door. It was dark as well.

She sat on a bench and let her sadness and disbelief wash over her.

How could a simple wish have created such chaos?

And had she been entirely wrong?

Angie remembered coming home that night, hoping someone had picked up some of the never-ending tasks. How could they not have seen that it wasn't a suggestion?

Maybe she did have the right to a quiet space, where everything was in place, just for a moment.

In any case, she wasn't going to find it here, because the mall was closing too, a lone employee hovering near the door, radiating impatience. Probably he was eager to go back to his family.

Angie wished him Merry Christmas as she walked out, and his stance relaxed, his smile genuine as he said it back.

If only everything could be this easy.

She walked across the parking lot and crossed the street into a park with a playground that was abandoned at the moment. She and Neva had taken Christina, and then Fiona and Elsa, here many times. The twins, of course, still loved to go. Angie sat down in one of the swings even though it was snowing. She had happy memories of this place, but it felt incredibly lonely now.

Perhaps she hadn't made it clear enough how much that quiet space mattered to her? Did it still matter, when her wish had caused so many misunderstandings?

And she might have been guilty of forgetting, just for a second or so, that she already had everything she'd ever dreamed of.

Her boss had given her time off. All she had to do was ask.

Neva's parents had joined them, and her own would have if she'd asked sooner. They didn't demand perfect, just wanted to enjoy time with their daughters and granddaughters.

Neva loved her.

Where did that leave Angie?

What was the conclusion she needed to draw?

She had tried and failed to undo her wish multiple times. Angie cast a look at her phone, her chest tightening when she realized it was only twenty minutes to midnight.

The mall closed at nine! How could she have been out here this long and not notice it?

Her fingers were ice cold, and when she checked the pockets of her coat, she realized she didn't have gloves with her. She felt cold inside out. What more could she do to fix this?

And no one believed her that this other life had even existed, well, no one except...

"Angie, hi."

Startled by the voice addressing her, she all but jumped from the swing and spun around, realizing that Nadine had been standing behind her. Where had she come from?

And perhaps there was no point in asking herself that. A wish granter. Was that some kind of Christmas elf?

Was she losing it?

"Hello. Nadine, look—" She stopped. What else could she say to her? Nadine wouldn't or couldn't help her. At least, she wouldn't provide Angie with a solution, and she couldn't seem to find one on her own.

"I didn't expect to see you tonight, but since you're here...Merry Christmas."

Nadine's tone was friendly, as if nothing strange had happened between them, as if it was perfectly normal that they were both here on Christmas Eve.

But that was exactly the problem, wasn't it? They shouldn't be. Nadine had to be aware that Angie's Christmas was anything but merry so far.

"Is it, though?"

"You tell me." She was still wearing the same guileless smile, telling Angie that her words weren't meant to be sarcastic. "I hope Neva liked her gift," she added, still wearing that guileless smile.

"I haven't given it to her yet," Angie confessed. "Is that even still real? Or will it disintegrate after midnight like the rest of my life?"

A patient, knowing expression appeared on the jeweler's face.

"Nothing will disintegrate. But you made a wish. Think about it. No one wishes for a life they hate, do they?"

"But here I am, all alone in the park on Christmas Eve. All I wanted was—"

That moment, Angie made peace with the fact that Nadine wouldn't give her an easy answer, or any answer, no matter how many times she asked for it. And perhaps that was the point.

Nadine was right.

She had made that wish.

What exactly was it that she wanted? Angie wondered. Then. Now. Not for Neva to give up her dream, not for Christina to attend an expensive school where she wasn't happy, not—

Angie checked her watch only to realize that she had seven minutes left. Likely, that wasn't enough time to change anything—or was it? What if everything stayed the way it was now?

Her mind was running through a slideshow of memories new and old, falling in love with Neva who approached life with so much more openness and less anxiety, their wedding day, their beautiful family growing, their children's milestones. Holidays celebrated together. The occasional argument, worries, plans postponed.

The hands of her clock moved forward. Nothing, she realized, would stop time from moving forward. Christmas Day was almost here.

Her heart had stopped pounding, and Angie was stunned to realize that her mind was calm and clear all of a sudden, the images, all of them, comforting. Even if some of them were more recent, coming from this new unfamiliar reality.

"I have to go now," Nadine said softly and touched her arm before she turned around and left.

"Wait!" Jolted into motion, Angie got to her feet and hurried after her so quickly she nearly slipped in the fresh snow.

Nadine halted and faced her again. "Is there something you wanted to say?"

"Yes. Yes, there is. Two minutes left. You're right. I made a wish, and I caused some, I don't know, disturbance in the universe, but you know what? Christina, Elsa, and Fiona are my kids, and Neva is my wife, and I love them more than anything is this world, or any world, for that matter. So, this is it. If this is the reality I must live in, then I will. It'll be okay, because we're together."

Nadine waited until Angie ran out of breath, and a distant church bell announced that it was Christmas Day.

"What am I doing? All I want for Christmas is to be home with my family. That's where I'm going now."

Nadine gave her another one of those gentle smiles. She hugged Angie and, without further words, walked away.

Angie returned to her car, sat inside, and turned on the radio.

She had never felt more at peace.

Chapter Sixteen

NEVA

"That was a long time ago when we had our two dogs, Ernie and Bert," Fiona explained to her grandmother, and Neva was jolted out of her state of scared disbelief.

It didn't have to mean anything. A long time ago for Fiona could mean something that had happened a year or two ago, or something she had imagined in pre-school age. Both Fiona and Elsa had vivid imaginations.

But she said this with so much sincerity, and Neva had to think of Angie's off timeline when it came to Fluffy, and the mention of another pet.

With the clock creeping closer to midnight, that magic moment, she couldn't help wondering if for some inexplicable reason, she had been the one who'd been wrong all along. She thought of the sketchbook she had found, pages after pages of their lives. Happy lives.

It was scary to think that her own memory had betrayed her, but what if this told them that they needed to find middle ground more often?

Angie clearly thrived on Christmas, and perhaps they had scaled it down too much in the past years, too worried about adding stress to the holidays when their lives were already so busy. They might have overlooked something.

She would have loved to pick up painting again, but Neva hadn't even considered this to be an option in recent years. And Christina...Neva blinked back tears thinking about their conversation. She had held something back that had been weighing on her.

It shouldn't be that way.

Neva wanted them to spend more time together. This was what they had been working for so hard. And yet she was here, while Angie had felt the need to leave...

This wasn't right. It was Christmas after all, and maybe to make it right, she had to believe.

"I'm going to check on Angie," she told her father and silently left the house.

Three minutes before Christmas Day, starting her car, Neva made a wish.

Chapter Seventeen

ANGIE

W hen Angie woke, the sun was shining into the window, the sky a brilliant blue just as predicted for Christmas Day. She sat up in bed, trying hard not to let panic take over. Christmas morning already.

She had missed dinner and gift giving, worrying everyone.

She could hear the sound of the shower. Was Neva mad at her for ruining everyone's evening? If nothing had changed, she would have to start with lots of apologies for this version of her family.

Determined to remain in the resolve she had somehow found last night, she slipped out of bed, shivering when she realized she didn't remember how she got into her pajamas—or even, how she got home. She couldn't bring herself to dwell on this for the moment.

After she put on her slippers, Angie quietly went downstairs, intending to get the coffee started. Instead, she started opening cupboards, took some milk out of the fridge and began preparing hot chocolate for everyone to the Christmas playlist on her phone. They had all earned something sweet. When it was done, she poured herself a mug and dropped a few small marshmallows in it.

Angie took a sip, her eyes welling up when the sweet taste and warmth of the beverage unleashed another flood of happy memories. Her parents had often made hot chocolate on Christmas morning when she was little. Later she and Neva had shared the sweet beverage during the holiday when they started living together, and of course they had continued that tradition with their children.

She went into the living room, stopping cold. Lots of unopened presents sat under the tree. A tree that looked a bit more crooked than she remembered. What had happened yesterday? Did everyone just go to bed without opening the gifts? Why? Did they want to wait for her?

Why couldn't she remember? Did she get drunk, or...Did Nadine's brand of magic have anything to do with it?

"Good morning, love. Merry Christmas."

She spun around, nearly spilling her beverage. Neva was smiling like she was happy to see her, carrying a mug of her own.

"You made hot chocolate," she added. "I didn't know it was possible, but now I love you even more."

"Not as much as I love you." They shared a smile, and Angie held the gaze of the woman she had shared her life with for almost two decades before she glanced over at the tree again and nearly dropped her mug. The ornaments Christina and the twins had made were back! In fact, the tree was decorated in their typical eclectic style, treasures from Angie's family and hers, and some that they had collected over time.

The rainbow heart ornament with the words *Love is Love* on it. A baby carriage that Angie's parents had given them when

Christina was on the way. Stars, apples, two dachshunds and a kitten.

Two? Did that mean...

"I'm so sorry. About everything," she blurted out. "I never meant to be ungrateful."

Neva stepped close to hug her.

"Angie, where is this coming from? It's all good. I'm sorry I didn't go out to buy more wrapping paper, but I found a few more rolls in the basement. It turns out we had more than enough for the rest of the presents."

"The rest of the..."

"Yeah, we should have more than enough time, and it's early. You could even get another batch of cookies in the oven if you wanted to." Neva winked. "Don't worry, you'll have lots of helpers. I talked to the girls, and they understand that if they want more sweets, they will have to lend a hand. We have our work cut out for tonight's dinner."

"Tonight's...I don't understand. What day is it?"

"What day?" Neva reached out to touch Angie's forehead, the gesture soft and tender. "Christmas Eve, of course. They day we've been waiting for! And If I have to keep your gift to myself much longer, I'm going to burst."

"Wait. What?" Angie couldn't help the goofy smile that spread on her face. "It's Christmas Eve!"

"Yes, exactly. What did you think?"

"It's not important." She hugged Neva close and then pulled back to kiss her gently. What was meant as a sweet reassurance, turned a little more passionate soon, until footsteps alerted them to the presence of another occupant in the house.

A yawning Christina stood in front of them, managing to roll her eyes at the same time. Said eyes lit up when she saw the tree with the gifts underneath.

"Wow, there are so many more. You did all of that last night?"

"Your moms are a whole lot more efficient than you think," Neva said with a wink. "But we really could use your help after breakfast."

"Of course. I look forward to seeing Grandmas and Grandpas again."

Me too, Angie thought. *Me, too.* She had to check.

"Let's make breakfast, shall we? We talk about Caron later."

"Caron?" Christina asked, frowning. "I thought we already had. I'm not transferring. Ashley doesn't like it there. Her parents think about pulling her out."

"Oh. Okay."

Could this be true? Did she really have her life back?

"I can start the pancakes," Christina offered. "We're having pancakes, right?"

"Absolutely." Angie hugged her too, until her daughter gently protested.

Her eyes were welling up again, and she suspected it would happen many more times today. And tomorrow.

Next, Fiona and Elsa, awake and excited, came rushing into the living room, equally excited furbabies in their wake.

Fluffy. And Bert *and* Ernie.

Angie crouched down only to have Bert and Ernie pad over to her while Fluffy seemed to find the tree and the packages underneath more interesting.

"Oh no!" Neva told her and rushed after the errant kitten.

"Look at all the gifts!" Fiona exclaimed while Christina smiled affectionately at her younger sister.

Angie petted the two dachshunds.

"Good to have you all back," she whispered and got to her feet, her heart full with gratitude and love for every person and being in this house. She had been given another chance. She was going to make it count.

THE PERFECT CHRISTMAS

·♥·♥·♥·♥·♥·

The day was busy, but surprisingly easily manageable with everyone having their assigned task. Angie's parents would take the guest room.

Neva had cleaned up her studio to make room for her parents' overnight stay. Even though there was a lot to do, Angie couldn't help but stare and wonder at the multiple canvases. So, Neva had picked up painting again. No, she reminded herself. She was back home, in the reality where Neva had never stopped.

Throughout the day, the girls were happy to help, or on occasion watch the pets if they got too intrigued by decorations or human food.

They sang Christmas carols, at times off-key enough to make everyone crack up.

When their guests arrived, and they sat down for a wintery cocktail, the non-alcoholic version for the girls, Angie learned that her parents were going on a cruise after all, a few days after Christmas.

"We would have never missed this," her mother said, beaming as one twin sat on either side of her. They'd receive their gifts later, but of course there were some chocolates to be unwrapped right away.

"I'm so glad you're here." Angie was in danger of tearing up again, but they were all happy tears this time. Fluffy was curled up next to her. No more cat allergy.

Over the course of the evening, she marveled at the life she had, that she and Neva had chosen together. They were raising smart and kind children, along with a some mostly well-behaved pets in a loving environment. Their respective parents got along great.

Today had been busy, but everyone had done their share.

The differences might be subtle, but she could see them, feel them.

They were happy again, even more than before.

After a scrumptious meal, they came to what was the most exciting part for their daughters. It was exciting for Angie, too, because there was quite a story attached to her gift for Neva.

"This is so beautiful! I love it."

Angie helped her put on the necklace, and yes, it was beautiful, but much more so on the woman she loved.

"Thank you so much. This is exactly like the one we saw..."

"Earlier this fall. I noticed that you liked it."

Neva smiled widely. "I was quite obvious about it, wasn't I? Well, I have something for you that I hope you like."

"I'm sure I will."

"Moms," Fiona and Elsa scolded in unison, curious and eager for them to continue.

Neva's gift was a wrapped envelope, and Angie made a show out of removing the bow slowly.

"Yes, Moms, get going," her father joked.

"Come on. It's Christmas. Let's enjoy the moment, okay?"

Finally, she revealed the red envelope and opened it. What she saw made her jaw drop.

"Neva. This is too much."

Can we afford it?

"No, it's not. You work so hard to make everyone happy, not just at Christmas, and you should know that we are aware of it, and we don't take you for granted."

It was on the tip of her tongue to say, *I never thought that*, but she just smiled, thinking back to the moment when she left the park in a different reality, wishing...

It had all come true.

"Thank you so much. This is wonderful," she said instead.

"You're going to have a lovely time," Laura, Neva's mom, said. "You've earned this, and I'm happy for you."

"We knew about it," Fiona said, "and Christina did too. It was hard not to tell, but we kept it a secret." She seemed very proud of it.

Angie looked around the room, everyone she held dear, with her on this day, in a home that held lots of memories, laughter and love. Who cared that the tree was a tiny bit crooked, or that they had "only" managed to do three kinds of cookies? They had each other, and a family that supported them.

They supported *her*, even when her wish for the perfect Christmas led to long to-do lists.

They *were* her perfect Christmas.

This was the life she had always dreamed of, and it was right here.

She had not failed.

All of a sudden, it all made sense.

"You are amazing. I love you. And I think it's time for a toast," she said. "To family. And love."

Everyone joined in, the girls with their non-alcoholic drinks.

Bert and Ernie barked, wanting to take part in the conversation, and Fluffy went after a low-hanging Christmas ornament.

Miraculously, Angie didn't feel the need to sneeze, panic or micromanage anymore. Christina picked up Fluffy and pointed her in the direction of a wrapped catnip pillow that held the kitten's attention for the moment.

"Merry Christmas," Angie said.

Neva's eyes sparkled with joy and pride as their glasses clinked together.

Miracles happened, and this family certainly was hers. It couldn't be a coincidence that she'd married a woman whose name meant snow...

A woman who had tirelessly plotted with their kids and parents to give Angie the most romantic gift she could have ever imagined.

"I love you," she whispered.

"I love you too. And I can't wait to take you away."

Angie still loved her family the most, but Christmas, all its magic included, would always be a close second.

Epilogue

ANGIE

The kids had been taken out by sheer exhaustion after a long day of waiting and traveling. Neva had been on a plane before, and she had no trouble falling asleep on the red-eye flight. It was all new for Angie who was taking in every moment with awe...That, and there was no way she could fall asleep to the sound of the plane.

Everything had happened so fast, and here they were, on their way to a romantic getaway to Paris. It would be an inspiration for Neva.

Angie, on the other hand, was constantly inspired by the woman by her side, but she also couldn't wait to see landmarks, museums, and quaint cafés.

When her gaze fell on the flight attendant quietly walking the isle, Angie could feel her jaw drop. This couldn't be...

She had wanted to leave a box of cookies for Nadine, but the house seemed empty when she went over, and she hadn't seen her since. Nadine, the jeweler and wish granter, who seemed to have a number of doppelgangers.

The woman walked by and smiled enigmatically. No, not a doppelganger. This *was* Nadine, who looked as serene and happy as Angie felt.

How was that possible?

She walked the length of the plane, then returned with a cart, handing out drinks and bags of pretzels with a small napkin.

When Angie unfolded it, the words *I knew you'd figure out what to do* were written on it.

The truth was, Angie hadn't done that much. She remembered Nadine saying that no one wished for something they hated. The moment she let go of her frantic activity and micromanaging, she had realized that she could make herself at home in whatever reality, as long as the ones she loved were with her. It was all that mattered, at Christmas, and all year.

She wouldn't get lost in the details anymore. If she needed help, she'd ask for it.

Angie leaned back and reached for Neva's hand and closed her eyes.

Just before she fell asleep to dreams of family gatherings, cookie baking, and Paris streets, her mind went back to the curious time when everything seemed out of order, and out of her control. She was certain that Neva's love, more than anything, had brought her home.

She understood it now. After all, Nadine had said that wishes could interact.

The rest, they might never know, and that was part of the magic of Christmas.

It was already perfect—and it always had been.

About the Author

B arbara Winkes writes sapphic crime drama and Christmas romance. She loves writing characters who get the job done, whether it's stopping a predator or saving cherished traditions—while still making time for love. She lives with her wife in Quebec City.

barbarawinkes.com

Also by Barbara Winkes

Bells Will Be Ringing
A Girlfriend for Christmas
Christmas Cupid
Destination Christmas, Next Stop Love
The Christmas Memory
The Wishing Tree